Penguin Books
Doctor on Toast

Richard Gordon was born in 1921. He has been an anaesthetist at a big London hospital, a ship's surgeon, and an assistant editor of a medical journal. He left medical practice in 1952 and started writing his 'Doctor' series. He is a member of the Surrey Cricket Club, and is married to a doctor. They have four children and live in a Victorian house in South London.

Richard Gordon

Doctor on Toast

Penguin Books
in association with Michael Joseph

Penguin Books Ltd, Harmondsworth,
Middlesex, England
Penguin Books, 625 Madison Avenue,
New York, New York 10022, U.S.A.
Penguin Books Australia Ltd, Ringwood,
Victoria, Australia
Penguin Books Canada Ltd, 2801 John Street,
Markham, Ontario, Canada L3R 1B4
Penguin Books (N.Z.) Ltd, 182–190 Wairau Road,
Auckland 10, New Zealand

First published by Michael Joseph 1961
Published in Penguin Books 1968
Reprinted 1970, 1971, 1975, 1977

Made and printed in Great Britain by
C. Nicholls and Company Ltd
Set in Monotype Baskerville

I

'Dr Grimsdyke,' announced our pretty little receptionist, 'there's a man behaving very strangely in the waiting-room.'

'Oh, really?' I glanced from the racing page of the morning paper. 'What's he doing? Laughing over the back numbers of *Punch*?'

'No, he's all alone, standing in front of the mirror making faces.'

'Good Lord!' I looked alarmed. 'Not likely to become violent, I hope?'

It was a beastly foggy December afternoon, when you could imagine Jack the Ripper still lurking in the London shadows or Holmes and Watson rattling by in a hansom to Baker Street. There were only ten of those shopping days left until Christmas, the stores were sprinkled with Santas and the pubs festooned with paper chains and the good wishes of the management, and I'd just moved into Park Lane as locum tenens to Dr Erasmus Potter-Phipps.

'Dear boy, I'm absolutely desperate for a holiday,' he'd explained when we met a few days before in the locker room at Sunningdale. 'The practice is really becoming too much for me.'

He idly flicked a driver.

'You know how one's female patients do so tend to fall in love with one? It's perfectly harmless, of course. One needn't fall in love with *them*, and it does their nerves the power of good. But this young actress I've been treating for mental prostration – you may have noticed in the papers? – has a husband with a positive persecution mania. It's all terribly tiresome, particularly as I imagined the fellow was climbing the Himalayas. So inconsiderate of him to arrive home without cabling first. The shock quite put the poor dear's case back several weeks.'

He inspected the head of his putter.

'Loath as I am to suspend treatment, I thought I might take a little holiday abroad. A few weeks' ski-ing does one the world of good at this time of the year. But the trouble is finding a suitable locum. You realize, dear boy, that I have a rather special sort of practice?'

I nodded. Razzy Potter-Phipps had in his time diagnosed half *Debrett*.

'All the young men are perfectly impossible these days. The hospitals don't seem to teach them anything but medicine. Why, the last locum I had performed a most embarrassing examination on a duchess. But if you happened yourself to be footloose and fancy free professionally ...?'

'Rely on me, old lad,' I'd agreed at once.

I'd a soft spot for Razzy, who'd often obliged with useful jobs, loans, or racing tips in the past. Besides, Christmas was coming, and finding the Grimsdyke coffers unseasonably low.

'Dear boy, I'm eternally grateful. Do move into my flat and draw anything you want from the petty cash. We can settle the details over a decent dinner when I get back in the New Year. So undignified, don't you think, for gentlemen to discuss money in public?'

But I'd hardly been in Potter-Phipps' Mayfair apartments long enough to discover which instrument cupboard he kept the sherry in when this maniac appeared. I glanced round the consulting room, which resembled a cross between the Messel suite at the Dorchester and Constance Spry's showrooms, and felt it would never do having people running berserk in it.

'What's the patient look like?' I asked the little receptionist.

'Oh, perfectly respectable otherwise, Doctor. He's about your age, very well dressed.' She smiled. 'Quite tall, dark, and handsome, in fact.'

'And making faces in mirrors ...?'

A slumbering memory gently creaked the bed of my subconscious.

'He doesn't happen to have side-whiskers, suède boots, a red carnation, and an Old Harrovian tie?' I added quickly.

'How very odd, Doctor! But certainly the side-whiskers and carnation –'

I gave a laugh. 'Kindly show Mr Basil Beauchamp inside.'

I hadn't seen Basil Beauchamp – pronounced Beecham – since the days I shared the same digs as a medical student, when I remembered he was always broke and the landlady had to send her daughter to her auntie's. But anyone who'd ever had the misfortune to live across the same landing could easily diagnose the mirror antics as his normal behaviour – the poor fellow's trouble was being an actor, and like all actors he somehow could never switch himself off. Very difficult it had been in the evenings, too, trying to learn up all that stuff for the examinations with Othello carrying on in the bedroom next door. And even when I lent him a bob for his gas meter to get a little peace, the next week he was generally Henry V, who, of course, is even noisier.

'Great heavens!' Basil himself appeared in the consulting room doorway, looking as usual like a combined effort by Savile Row and the Burlington Arcade. 'It's Gaston Grimsdyke!'

'What ho, old lad,' I greeted him. 'It seems a long time since we used to pinch each other's bathwater.'

He stood staring at me, like Macbeth when Banquo came to dinner.

'But – but what on earth are *you* doing here? Where's Dr Potter-Phipps?'

'Enjoying a well earned Christmas holiday at St Moritz,' I explained. 'I'm obliging as his locum tenens.'

'What? You mean you actually became a qualified doctor in the end?' He gave a loud laugh. 'Well, well! How extraordinary.'

I felt slightly nettled at this remark, but remembering that actors have a peculiar sense of humour waved him to a chair affably enough.

'How about you, Basil?' I offered Potter-Phipps' silver cigarette-box. 'Abandoned those big dreams of fame and fortune on the boards?'

Come to think of it, I hadn't even heard of the chap since he had a frightful row with the gas-man over the shillings and suddenly left the digs, when all the time I'd been looking forward to seeing his name up in lights and getting free tickets for the London theatres.

'Of course I haven't given up the stage.' It was Basil's turn to be annoyed. 'Why, I'm turning down unsuitable parts every week.'

'Oh, sorry –'

'Not to mention opening in a new show immediately after Christmas.'

'Then rely on me to come along and clap you to the echo,' I told him, still thinking of those free seats.

'It – er, isn't in the West End, of course.' Basil shifted slightly. 'You've heard of Blackport-under-Tyne? Busy little place up north. Actually, it's pantomime. I'm the Demon King.'

'Pantomime?'

It seemed odd that the chap who could get half-way through *Coriolanus* in his bath on Sunday mornings should go scouring the country being demon kings.

'Yes, all very jolly and seasonable, you know. A chappie I met in a King's Road pub recommended Potter-Phipps,' he went on, changing the subject, 'though I must say I didn't expect anything quite so grand.' Basil stared round the consulting room. 'I suppose all your patients must be frightfully wealthy?'

'Not after they've paid the bills.'

'Well, it certainly does the heart good, dear chappie,' he continued, expanding rather, 'to meet you again in such prosperous surroundings.'

'Oh, I don't know. I think Razzy only gave me the job because he thought I'd go nicely with his furniture.'

'Ah! You were always so modest.'

'Come, come –'

'Yes, so modest. And so generous.'

He flicked ash over the Chippendale consulting desk.

'The dear old digs!' Basil blew a chain of smoke rings. 'We were great pals in those happy days, weren't we, Grim? Do you remember how I lent you my dress suit? And came down to let you in when you threw stones at my window?'

I agreed politely, though pretty sure I was the one with the dress suit. And as Basil slept like a churchyard, anyway, you wouldn't have got him down by throwing a brick at his window.

'In respect for this old friendship of ours,' he continued, 'I shall now be perfectly frank with you.'

'Oh, yes?'

Basil hesitated. 'Dear chappie, when I mentioned just then I was turning down parts every week, I was exaggerating rather. In fact, since we last met the parts I've been offered have kept up a steady average – between damn few and damn all. Believe me, Grim,' he added sombrely, 'I used to think the poor starving actor was just a comic character you met in books. Now I can assure you I know better.'

'I say, what tough luck.'

I felt genuinely sorry for the chap, particularly remembering how he used to angle for a second helping of pudding and swipe all the marmalade.

'Why else,' Basil demanded, jumping up and starting to pace Potter-Phipps' peach-coloured carpet, 'do you imagine I would descend to buffooning before a bunch of bilious brats? In a theatre whose usual entertainment consists in the disrobing of gangs of superannuated barmaids? Sheer necessity, dear chappie, that's why! Though mind you,' he added warmly, 'one still has one's professional pride. I'm going to play this Demon King as he's never been played before. You've heard of "The Method"? One *lives* one's part, day and night, awake and asleep. I've been feeling positively satanic for weeks.'

'Well, you've scared the life out of our receptionist for a start,' I consoled him.

'Meanwhile, of course, one must live.' He helped himself to another cigarette. 'One isn't paid by this stinking management for rehearsals. So I was wondering, on the strength of our long-standing chumminess, if you could advance me some small sum – say a hundred pounds . . . ?'

I gave a laugh.

'Basil, you idiot! Don't you see I'm only the locum here? The understudy,' I explained, as he was standing with his mouth open. 'All I get is a modest salary when Razzy Potter-Phipps gets fed up jumping off Swiss mountains. As a matter of fact,' I added, 'you looked so jolly smart when you showed up, and what with all my Christmas shopping to do, I'd half a mind to touch *you* for a bit yourself.'

'Me? Good God!'

He fell into his chair, looking shocked.

'But cheer up,' I went on, after a pause. 'You're always reading in the papers of stars being discovered overnight. And I bet all those posh actors with titles in London were demon kings themselves once. Or mere broker's men, if it comes to that.'

But Basil said nothing. He just sat shaking his head, looking as forlorn as a burnt-out firework.

'Alas, dear chappie,' he managed to say at last. 'Success is never as simple as that. It all comes back to this beastly business of money. If only I could afford to live at the right address! To be seen in the right places, to take the right people out to lunch at the right restaurants ... About my talent, of course, there is no doubt.'

'Of course not.' Knowing how he could expand on this topic, I added quickly, 'But what's the trouble that brings you here today?'

'I was almost forgetting.' Basil roused himself. 'I should like a complete physical examination, please. Can you oblige?'

'Naturally. But to what object? Life insurance? Emigration? Being a demon king all day wearing you out?'

'Neither.' He gave a little sniff at his carnation. 'I am going to be married.'

'Married? Congratulations.'

'I read somewhere that a medical examination was advisable in those contemplating matrimony, so here I am.'

I remembered he was also a shocking hypochondriac, always sneaking into my room to catch something new from Conybeare's *Medicine*.

'Though I suppose matrimony is about the most damn stupid thing I possibly *could* contemplate,' Basil continued gloomily. 'My entire worldly goods fitting comfortably into a couple of suitcases under the bed in my digs. You were perfectly right just now, Grim – I should have turned in the stage years ago for some nice steady lucrative job, like selling encyclopaedias at the door. But you know how it goes. No true actor ever gives his final performance until it's accompanied by flowers and slow music. Meanwhile, my hand has been accepted by the sweetest and most delightful person in the whole world – Ophelia O'Brien. You know her, of course.'

'I don't think I've had the honour –'

'She's the girl in the detergent advertisements on the sides of all the buses.'

'Ah, yes. The one with the snow-white whatsits.'

'But dear chappie, you shall meet her.' Basil suddenly brightened up. 'She's coming round in ten minutes to collect me.'

'In that case you'd better go behind the screen in the corner and take your shirt off,' I directed. 'And by the way, you needn't bother about the bill. You can have this one on the house.'

'How terribly good of you –'

'Regard it as a wedding present,' I told him.

I wasn't over-enthusiastic about meeting Basil's prospective missus. I've known a few models in my time, and though they look pretty smashing showing off tartan jodhpurs or whatever in *Vogue*, they generally turn out to be skinny girls with loud voices who keep borrowing fourpence off you to telephone their agents. It was therefore a nice surprise a few minutes later to be shaking hands with the most beautiful little blonde I had ever seen in my life.

2

'Are you perfectly sure you've completely recovered from your operation, Gaston?' asked my cousin, Miles Grimsdyke, F.R.C.S., the surgeon.

We were sitting in a couple of paper hats over the remains of the Christmas dinner, his wife Connie having retired to wipe more of it from the face of their two-year-old son.

Miles helped himself to more port. 'Last year you were quite the life and soul of the party –'

'And this one I've been sitting about uttering sighs deep enough to blow the pudding out,' I agreed.

'You have seemed far from your usual self, I must say. I think young Bartholomew was quite disappointed.'

I lit one of his cigars. 'Fact is, old lad, I find myself at the moment in a position of some embarrassment.'

'Indeed? I am sorry to hear it.' Miles pushed across the decanter. 'But as much as I should like to assist you, you must remember I have now a child to support. Believe me, the frightful cost of human reproduction –'

'My condition, alas, for once cannot be eased by the mere application of cash.'

He looked startled. 'You haven't done anything awful, have you? I mean, being drunk and disorderly? Or – Good heavens! – you haven't taken drugs?'

'I am in love.'

'Oh, is that all?'

'Well may you take the blasé view,' I admitted with a sigh. 'Of course, I've trifled with an affection or two in the past, in those jolly days when I used to push nurses home over the St Swithin's mortuary gate. But that was mere emotional chicken-pox. This is the acute full-blown complaint, with all complications.'

'H'm. What's the lucky lady's name?'

'Ah, yes.' I cracked a nut. 'I'm afraid I'm not just now at liberty to tell you. You see,' I explained, 'she happens to be engaged to somebody else.'

'And will you be invited to the wedding?'

I hadn't even taken the trouble of discovering Ophelia's telephone number. I'd taken a laboratory specimen from Basil in Razzy's consulting room that afternoon, and as he was catching the midnight train to rehearse in Blackport he suggested I rang his fiancée with the result. The following morning Ophelia and I became rather chatty on the wire, so I asked her out for a Yuletide drink, and the day after it was lunch, and the next evening dinner, and soon we were tooting round the night-clubs, and now I worshipped the very ground she dug her spiked heels into.

And all the time Basil was popping through trapdoors saying, 'Fe fi fo fum!' No wonder I felt a bit of a cad.

'It was perhaps not very kind of me to make that last remark,' Miles relented. 'Particularly in view of the season.'

'Oh, I don't know,' I conceded. 'After all, we Grimsdykes have our honour. Even our old grandpa who had such trouble with the servant problem, what with chasing all the housemaids round the attics.'

I could see Miles thought me a bit of a cad, too, and I could hardly blame him. My cousin was a severe little bristly chap, openly admitted in the family to have inherited my share of the brain-producing genes as well, and our relationship had been rather brittle since the day he caned me at school for filling his cricket boots with treacle. Though admittedly he'd become chummier since reaching the St Swithin's consultant staff and assuming all the trappings of a rising young London surgeon – a new Alvis, a plate in Welbeck Street, a nice wife, a blotter on half-a-dozen committee tables, and even a faintly disgusting disease named after him.

'At least I've managed so far to keep the family escutcheon as unspotted as a polar bear in a snowstorm,' I added a little defensively.

'That is true enough, Gaston. And certainly no one would be happier than Connie and myself if you did manage to settle down in a home of your own.' Miles reached for the port again. 'Particularly in view of the Prime Minister's letter to me last week.'

I looked up. 'Good Lord! He doesn't want you to stand for Parliament, or anything?'

'Oh, tut!' said Miles, though not seeming displeased at the idea. 'But he *does* want me to join the Wincanton commission in the New Year.'

I wondered quickly if that was the one inquiring into conditions in the Stock Exchange or conditions in prisons.

'The Royal Commission on the State of Public Morality,' Miles explained, looking smug under his paper hat. 'I'm sure even you will appreciate this is a great honour. Though I fear it will be hard work. We shall be obliged to investigate nude spectacles, to mix with women of the lowest morals, and penetrate some of the foulest drinking dens in London.'

It all sounded jolly good fun to me, but remembering how seriously Miles took his welfare work even as a medical student, I simply congratulated him.

'I particularly wish to make a success of the appointment,' Miles continued, half to himself. 'For who knows where it might lead? One might become Dean of the Hospital . . . Vice-Chancellor of the University . . . a Fellow of All Souls . . . a Life Peer . . .'

The chap was full of port, of course.

'I gather you are undertaking Sir Lancelot Spratt's biography?' he added, remembering himself.

'As a matter of fact, I'm going round tomorrow to start sorting the stuff. He's such a busy fellow it seems Boxing Day's the only time he has to spare.'

I found myself writing Sir Lancelot's biography through having recently published a novel, which enjoyed modest success among all those people who can't yet afford television sets. Basil hadn't heard of it, of course, but then no actors ever read books. And apart from unexpected emergencies presented by train smashes or Razzy's love life, I had – like Drs Anton Chekhov and John Keats before me – abandoned the healing art for the literary life.

Being a literary gent certainly has its advantages, such as not needing to shave before starting work in the mornings and all the literary luncheons sitting at the top table, which has the flowers and the buckshee booze. But there are snags. First of all, of course, you have to write more ruddy books. Then what with rubbing shoulders with the latest angry young chaps, or signing copies of the Works in bookshops, and holding forth over the cheese at those luncheons, you tend to develop the well-known clinical condition of *megalocrania acuta*. It's just the same the day you pass your finals and qualify, and go charging round the hospital in the biggest stethoscope out of John Bell and Croyden's, trying to get everybody to call you 'Doctor'.

In hospital you're fortunately cured pretty smartly by the ward sisters, who can deflate young doctors as easily as a kid popping soap-bubbles. But in the literary life Fate is left with the job. It was a pretty bumptious Grimsdyke who returned from a trip to New York on his proceeds, when Fate neatly stuck a foot in his path. I arrived in London to find the publishers' shutters up and the beastly chaps gone bankrupt, which was particularly awkward as I'd asked the air hostess out to lunch, and all I had in the world was one of those little cellophane bags of airsick barley-sugar.

I'd managed to scrape up enough to take a houseboat off Chelsea and start another novel, which I didn't expect would knock spots off Tolstoy, but might cheer up some of the fierce gents who go sniping through the literary jungle on Sunday mornings. But Fate, not having the advantage of an English education, doesn't recognize the code of never kicking a man when he's down. I hadn't got farther with the novel than cleaning all the letters in my typewriter with a pin, when I was carted into St Swithin's with a pretty nasty appendix. As usual among doctors, everyone misdiagnosed the case and if they hadn't finally sent for Sir Lancelot Spratt I'd have been having a pretty chilly Christmas of it, perched on the edge of a cloud fooling about with a harp.

'I trust you are being a satisfactory patient, Grimsdyke?' Sir Lancelot had said, appearing in the ward a few days after the operation to inspect his handiwork. 'They say that doctors invariably make the worst ones.'

'I'm learning all sorts of things about hospitals I never knew before, sir,' I replied, lying among the grapes and chrysanthemums.

He nodded. 'You have discovered the only way. It would, for instance, do the Bar a power of good if more barristers than at present served a spell in jail. Sister,' he added, as she replaced my bedclothes, 'I believe I left my notebook in your office. Would you have the kindness to fetch it?'

The surgeon stood for a moment stroking his beard.

'Now we have a few seconds alone, young man,' he went on, 'I have the chance to ask your help in a matter of some delicacy.'

'Mine, sir?'

I stared at him. In the days when I was one of his students, I suppose Sir Lancelot had thrown at me practically everything nasty that came conveniently to hand in his operating theatre. I now felt he was like Bobby Locke asking his caddy to drive off for him in the Open.

'I should like you to be my ghost.'

'Your what, sir?'

'I believe that is the technical term? But we must be brief. Your cousin Miles and my colleagues in the hospital are pressing me to write my memoirs. I have had a not uninteresting life, and they imagine the publication might in some way raise the present lamentable standing of our profession in the eyes of the British public. We are, alas, no longer tin gods. And we are very far from being the gold-plated tin gods of our American colleagues. Be that as it may. I could, of course, perfectly well write the book myself if I had the time. But these days I have no longer the leisure even to send up my cases to the *Lancet*, particularly as I have recently been appointed consultant to the Police Welfare Club.'

'Congratulations, sir,' I remarked.

'Thank you, Grimsdyke. The duties are arduous and rather unexciting – policemen for some reason run largely to varicose veins and hernias – but it throws me a good deal with our own famous pathologist. Dr McFiggie is, of course, the President. He very courteously allowed me to see the Bayswater victim in the mortuary this morning. I must confess,' Sir Lancelot added, noticing my paperback mystery from the ward library, 'I find the study of homicide utterly fascinating. I should write a book about that, too, if only I had the time.' He sighed briefly. '"The wisdom of a learned man cometh by opportunity of leisure: and he that hath little business shall become wise". You are familiar with Ecclesiasticus? In short, I should be much obliged if you would accept the task of my biography. There will of course be a small honorarium – shall we say fifty guineas?'

This was a bit of a poser. If I pottered through Sir Lancelot's memoirs for a mere fifty quid, not only would the world have to resign itself to waiting for the novel but the landlord of the houseboat would have to do the same about his rent. I stared for a moment through the ward windows, where the last leaves on the dusty plane trees in the courtyard were gold-plated by the afternoon autumn sun. Soon everything would be fairylights and mistletoe, then it would be daffodils and the Boat Race and asparagus and cricket, and in no time summer and Ascot and strawberries and cream again, and if life looked pretty good I remembered it now came with the compliments of Sir Lancelot Spratt.

'It would be an honour, sir,' I said.

'Excellent. I suggest you start work about Christmas time, when I can supply you at my house with all the necessary papers. I really must apologize,' he added, as Sister hurried up, 'I seem to have my notebook in my pocket all the while.'

It was when first trying out Sir Lancelot's stitches that I ran into Razzy, then of course I met Ophelia, and Christmas found me mooching through the general jollity in Miles' house thinking less of Sir Lancelot's life than the way the little soft hairs curled at the base of her neck.

'I sincerely hope your affair with this lady does not end discreditably,' observed Miles across the table, after chatting for a while about the memoirs and I fancy trying to drop the hint I might include a few words about himself.

'The situation has happened to chaps before now, of course,' I told him. 'Romeo, for instance.'

'I certainly hope it won't finish as disastrously as that.' Miles looked a bit alarmed. 'Perhaps,' he added, with one of his looks, 'on the strength of my long experience in welfare work among broken homes you will allow me to offer you a little sensible advice –'

But at that moment Connie came in, and we both had to go out and be bears.

3

The following afternoon I drove the 1930 Bentley across the empty streets of London, while the population lay recovering from its annual twenty-four hours' attempt at committing mass digestive suicide.

I'd spent Boxing Day morning in Park Lane treating the first post-festive dyspepsias, though the practice was pretty slack because Razzy's patients were mostly hurtling down Swiss slopes themselves or floundering in goggles round Jamaica pretending they were fish. I'd plenty of time to think about Ophelia, and pretty miserable it made me, too – come to think of it, the old passion is far from a light-hearted matter of a hey, and a ho, and a hey nonino. In its more virulent form it can make you feel pretty rotten, like the flu. Particularly as Ophelia had disappeared for a whole week to the dear old people miles away in the country, and all I'd got left was her photograph showing off latest creations in the waiting-room magazines, for some odd reason always slap in the middle of the Piccadilly traffic or surrounded by lots of empty milk bottles and dustmen. As for Basil, I reflected sourly as I drove round Marble Arch, the chap was at that very moment sticking on his forked tail and whiskers and preparing to shoot into the public eye through his trap-door up in Blackport.

Sir Lancelot seemed to live in some style. A pretty Italian maid in a frilly apron took my overcoat, and he appeared himself to lead me upstairs to the study of his Harley Street house. These days you don't expect to find consultants living in Harley Street, of course, any more than you expect to find bankers dossing down in the City. In fact, from the brass plates clustered round the door-posts like cottage roses you can tell that those tall elegant consulting rooms and tall elegant receptionists are all shared among several chaps. But Sir Lancelot maintained that no surgeon could possibly remain a gentleman and live in Wimbledon, though not mentioning quite so often that he'd bought up the mews behind his house years ago, and was making a packet letting it out as garages.

His study was furnished in the style popular among Victorian headmasters, and the leather-topped desk covered with bundles of yellow papers and stacks of faded photographs, which struck me as having no interest to anybody except the St Marylebone Refuse Department.

'You will forgive me for leaving you,' Sir Lancelot apologized, 'but I have an important speech to prepare for the Royal College of Surgeons downstairs. Just leaf your way through my papers. You will no doubt discover a skeleton or two in my cupboard, but I can assure you that the cupboards of many colleagues at St Swithin's resemble osteological museums.'

I hadn't got further with the job than trying to spot whether Sir Lancelot was the pimply chap holding the ball in the picture of the local football team, when the door opened and Lady Spratt appeared.

'My dear Gaston! We did so miss you at the hoop-la this year.'

'What ho, there,' I greeted her, 'I missed it myself. Just when I was getting my eye in for those little china dogs, too.'

'I've brought you a nice cup of tea,' she announced. 'I'm sure you'll need it after all your hard work.'

Anyone at St Swithin's would have imagined that Sir Lancelot had a wife resembling Boadicea, but Lady Spratt was a little fluffy thing as vague as the middle of a soufflé. We'd become chummy over the years, running the St Swithin's winter theatricals or the St Swithin's summer fête, and jolly useful it had been sometimes to dilute the fire and brimstone Sir Lancelot kept by the bucket for delinquent students.

'I'm so glad you are writing Lancelot's life,' she added, fluttering a bit.

'Worthy of a Boswell, I assure you.'

'But first of all –' Lady Spratt shot a glance towards the

door. ‘I wonder if I might ask you a special favour?’ There was a pause. ‘In fact, I am going to ask your help, Gaston, in a matter of great delicacy.’

I felt confused. As far as the Spratts were concerned, Grimsdyke seemed to be turning into everybody’s auntie.

‘But what on earth about?’

‘About this ghastly crime business.’

‘Crime business?’ I wondered if she’d been embezzling the hoop-la takings.

‘My husband,’ she explained. ‘Have you noticed he has been behaving oddly recently?’

Of course, Sir Lancelot had been behaving oddly for years. But some of our greatest surgeons were shocking eccentrics, and though he didn’t measure up to the eighteenth century ones with their gold-headed canes, Sir Lancelot was as unusual among London consultants as a bottle of champagne at breakfast.

‘Ever since he was appointed to that Police Club,’ Lady Spratt continued, ‘he’s been totally unable to talk about anything unconnected with sudden death, which is really quite unhealthy, not to mention extremely boring in the evenings.’

‘He just takes an enthusiastic interest in everything he meets,’ I murmured. After all, chaps must stand together, whoever they are.

‘And don’t I know it.’ She perched on the edge of his desk. ‘Last year it was the ballet, when I was forced to entertain all those peculiar young men and women. The year before it was racehorses, which thank heavens was too expensive to last. Now he follows all the murders like an errand boy, and is quite making himself the laughing stock of St Swithin’s – or so the Professor’s wife troubled to tell me in a loud voice right in the middle of Harrods. It really won’t do, if he wants to be the next President of the Royal College of Surgeons. And worst of all, he’s made a bosom friend of that rude little man with dirty fingernails, McFiggie.’

I could agree that Dr Angus McFiggie was rude. Most pathologists are, probably from never having to make light conversation with their patients. He was a little red-faced

Aberdonian with eyebrows like Highland bracken at the end of a hot summer, whom I'd often seen in his long red rubber apron busy in the new St Swithin's mortuary – which was about the most comfortable spot in the whole hospital, being all air-conditioning, strip lights, and white tiled walls, except for that oversized filing cabinet thing let into the far end.

'Not to mention keeping me awake half the night reading detective stories,' Lady Spratt ended. 'So I was wondering, Gaston, as you've known him so long at the hospital, if you could somehow suggest how to divert his energy elsewhere?'

This seemed a tall order. I was dutifully turning over the possibilities of stamp-collecting, country rambles, or a girl-friend, when the door suddenly opened and the surgeon appeared himself.

'Maud! What the devil have you done with my bedside reading lamp?' he asked, ignoring me.

'Your bedside lamp? I've moved it to one of the spare rooms.'

Sir Lancelot looked mystified. 'But what on earth for? You know how I like to read in bed. I was right in the middle of a rollicking good yarn about thugee, too.'

'Didn't I tell you?' Lady Spratt fitted a cigarette into her holder. 'My brother's arriving this week-end.'

'Maud, really!' The surgeon stamped his foot. 'You know perfectly well how I dislike people in the house. Life will be quite intolerable with the feller continually taking my favourite chair and all the hot water. You should have consulted me first.'

'Don't make a fuss, dear, *please*. Of course we have a moral obligation to put them up. Hotels in London are so frightfully expensive.'

'Them – ? Don't tell me he's bringing his blasted missus?'

'And his family, naturally.' Lady Spratt flicked her lighter. 'I thought it would be nice for them to see all the shops and theatres and things during the Christmas holidays.'

Sir Lancelot drew himself up. 'Then I shall spend the week-end at the club.'

'Very well dear.'

'That seems the most convenient solution for everyone,' he added, with his best bedside dignity.

'Not really, dear. You see, they will be staying for three weeks.'

'Three weeks? Good God!'

'Where are you going to?' demanded Lady Spratt.

'To lock up the cellar before I forget.'

'Really, Lancelot! Don't be ridiculous. You know my brother is most abstemious.'

'Rubbish! I've never met such a leech for the vintage port.'

'Which reminds me, I've arranged a little dinner party for Saturday –'

'Maud, this is absolutely preposterous! You've known for years how I detest entertaining out of the week –'

'You will join us, won't you, Gaston?' Lady Spratt added calmly. 'After all, you're almost one of the family now, aren't you?'

Ophelia still being away on Saturday, I accepted.

'I've asked Miss Gracie from the B.B.C., which still leaves me one man short. But I expect you will easily enough find someone interesting from the hospital, won't you, Lancelot? So glad you can come, Gaston. Black tie.'

4

Saturday was one of those Dickensian evenings when the street lamps throw a watery glow through the fog and the buses crawl past looking like great tanks of tropical fish. Though I'd have preferred to share chips out of the same newspaper as Ophelia, I put on a dinner jacket and drove from Razzy's flat to Harley Street, unable to help myself feeling pretty tickled. It seemed odd to be riding on the Spratt bandwagon, after Sir Lancelot had for years squashed me under the steamroller of his personality. Besides, it was well known in St Swithin's that the surgeon did himself well, and though Razzy had left the larder well stocked it's surprising how soon you can get fed up with a diet of *pâté de foie gras* and tinned lychees.

I rang the bell and the pretty Italian maid showed me into the drawing-room. Standing in front of the fire, his legs apart, smoking a pipe like a small tuba and generally making himself at home, was Sir Lancelot's brother-in-law.

'Good evening, my Lord,' I said.

'Ah, good evening, Doctor,' replied the Bishop of Wincanton.

Personally I don't mix much with Bishops, except during the Varsity rugger match at Twickenham, which must be the only time in the world you can find yourself standing in the gents' between a couple of them. Sir Lancelot's brother-in-law was himself one of the lean, athletic-looking sort, with a nose like a niblick and a chin like a bulldozer, and I remembered the limbs now cosy in gaiters had once appeared in little shorts to stroke a winning crew for Oxford.

'My wife,' said the Bishop.

She was one of those fragile-looking creatures who often attach themselves to muscular men, like the hook-worm.

'Sandra, my eldest daughter.'

Just like Mum, but more anaemic.

'My younger children.'

A shocking pair of about twelve, sitting in the corner surreptitiously picking their noses.

'And this is Miss Gracie,' added Lady Spratt, fluttering over the sherry.

She had a pink woollen dress, pale ginger hair, gold-rimmed glasses and rather careful vowel-sounds.

As for poor Sir Lancelot, for once he didn't seem to be in the room at all. He just sat in a chair, scowling at his relative's well-polished boots.

'As I was saying,' the Bishop continued, while I took the sofa next to Sandra. 'The pain commences immediately beneath the back collar-stud.'

'Presumably you mean the front collar-stud,' growled Sir Lancelot.

'I recall most vividly the sudden onset,' the Bishop went on, as the maid handed me a glass of sherry. 'I had just risen to address the luncheon marking the opening of the Assizes.'

'The Horse Show, Charles,' murmured his wife.

'The Assizes, my dear, I am positive,' returned the Bishop firmly. 'I assure you the agony was most acute. Naturally, one wonders if it might indicate something serious underneath –'

'Oh, that's very possible, very possible indeed,' agreed Sir Lancelot.

'You will no doubt recall, Lancelot, I told you of an exactly similar attack on the beach two summers ago.'

I didn't take long tumbling to it that the Bishop, like so many chaps who spend their youth hurling themselves across football fields or propelling themselves backwards up rivers, was a shocking hypochondriac. He was also one of these people who keep cadging medical advice, even if it is provided free these days like the school milk. I knew this habit made Sir Lancelot bristle all over, and he often carried on at St Swithin's about 'despicable professional shop-lifting.'

'My unfortunate wife,' the Bishop continued smoothly,

'suffers from severe indigestion. The pain, which is of a burning nature, comes on immediately before meals.'

'After meals, Charles.'

'Before meals, my dear, I think we decided. The pain, I will add, is situated just below the ribs, and is accompanied by considerable flatulence.'

'My God! Three weeks!' I heard Sir Lancelot mutter.

We all listened politely while the Bishop drew a neat clinical picture of a case of hysterical dyspepsia, and ended, 'What, my dear Lancelot, do you advise?'

'Consult a doctor,' replied the surgeon.

'Lancelot!' hissed Lady Spratt.

But before anyone could take this in, the maid opened the door again and announced, 'Dr Angus McFiggie.'

'My dear feller!' Sir Lancelot jumped up. 'I'm delighted you could get away. Let me introduce you to everybody. This is Dr McFiggie – *the* Dr McFiggie.'

I could see the guests were pretty impressed. After all, they were always seeing our pathologist in the Sunday papers on the scene of the most fashionable crimes in the country, and MCFIGGIE IN THE BOX on the placards could sell the evening papers like the result of the Derby. In St Swithin's itself, of course, his lectures were always crowded, particularly the one on rape, which was illustrated with lantern slides.

'And now I'm sure we shall all of us be most interested to hear Dr McFiggie's views on the Bayswater case,' continued Sir Lancelot proudly, glaring at the Bishop and settling his guest in the best chair.

'Um, yes,' said the Bishop vaguely.

'Personally, I am convinced the husband did it. Eh, McFiggie?'

But McFiggie only grunted and sucked sherry through his ginger moustache like bathwater draining out through the loofah. Although the chap could swap nasty remarks with Q.C.s, and even give Her Majesty's judges a comeback from the witness-box, it became clear as Sir Lancelot tried a few more openings that he was a shocking social failure. He just sat staring at his feet and working his eyebrows up and down, until they looked in danger of getting matted together permanently. I suppose he would have felt really at home in the room only if the lot of us had been dead.

'It is surely freely admitted inside our profession that many doctors murder their wives,' went on Sir Lancelot chattily. 'And that many more ought to.'

'There was Dr Crippen, sir,' I mentioned, to help the conversation. 'He put his under the cellar floor.'

'Exactly, Grimsdyke. And Dr Ruxton cut his up in the bath. You may not all be aware that the last Englishman to be hanged in public was one Dr Palmer, the poisoner? It was extremely embarrassing for his old hospital. For years afterwards they had to explain the poor fellow met his end while attending some sort of open-air meeting, when the platform suddenly collapsed beneath his feet.'

'Lancelot!' hissed Lady Spratt again.

The Bishop's wife then started telling everybody about the dyspepsia once again, McFiggie sat picking the soup stains off the lapels of his dinner jacket, and I tried chatting to Sandra about the ballet. On the whole, Lady Spratt looked pretty relieved when the maid reappeared to announce dinner.

'Our two youngest ones will now go to bed,' pronounced the Bishop, it seemed to everyone's agreement. 'They have an exciting day in store tomorrow. Their mother is taking them to the Zoological Gardens.'

'Which with any luck will keep them,' grunted Sir Lancelot.

The meal started very pleasantly, with Sir Lancelot expertly slitting the turkey to ribbons in a couple of minutes. Though I must say McFiggie didn't help much with the conversation, until Miss Gracie turned to him and said with a smile:

'Dr McFiggie, you look so very tired. I suppose like all doctors you've had a simply frantic day?'

The pathologist took another swig of Sir Lancelot's special burgundy and wiped his moustache.

'Up early,' he grunted.

'Some poor soul, I suppose,' chimed in the Bishop automatically, 'who needed your attention?'

'Exhumation job,' replied McFiggie.

Miss Gracie looked as though she'd found a slug in her Brussels sprouts.

'Indeed?' Sir Lancelot glanced from his plate at once. 'Anything interesting?'

'Aye.' McFiggie threw a quick look round the table. 'It's a woman they put under the sod the best part of a year ago. Usual thing, y'know. Anonymous letters, insurance claim, another woman, police get to hear.'

'My dear feller! I insist you tell us the full story at once.'

'Weel – I was down at the Yard last Tuesday, and the Superintendent said, "I suppose we'd better get her up, Doctor". So there I was, at five this morning in the cemetery.'

I noticed that everyone had stopped eating.

McFiggie gave a laugh. 'And it was that cold and dark we damn near started on the wrong one.'

I shot our pathologist a professional glance. Not only was he expanding under the influence of Sir Lancelot's burgundy, but I fancied the chap had been so overawed by the social ordeal he'd been stoking up for hours beforehand, like we did ourselves before the lemonade dances in the Nurses' Home.

'Errors are ever possible in your exacting professional duties,' murmured the Bishop after a moment.

'And my boots were leaking,' grumbled McFiggie. 'I usually keep a special pair for exhumations and the like, but I must have lost 'em.'

'But what did you discover, McFiggie?' insisted Sir Lancelot.

'Discover?' The pathologist banged the table. 'Plenty, believe you me. We got her out – coffin split open, o'course, always seem to these days – and I said, "Let me have a dekko at her." The Superintendent gave a wee laugh and said, "You won't see much, Doctor. Not from this smell." He's a comic card, the Super. Though he was right enough. Very low lying that cemetery. But I'll bet my last sixpence –' McFiggie banged the table again, knocking over a few glasses. 'The report on her guts tomorrow comes up with phosphorus poisoning.'

'Mummy, I think I've left my handkerchief upstairs,' said the Bishop's daughter.

'Now isn't that absolutely fascinating?' demanded Sir Lancelot.

'The resources of science in the preservation of law and order are indeed remarkable,' muttered the Bishop, quietly laying his knife and fork to one side.

'Aye, but if you want to hear something really good, your Reverence –'

'Are you interested in music, Dr McFiggie?' asked Lady Spratt.

'I'll tell you what I found this very night in Camden Town. It'll be all over the papers in the morning, anyway.'

As McFiggie paused to suck his teeth I felt the moment had come for a brilliant piece of sabotage by interrupting with a funny story. But I could only remember the old one about the Bishop and the parrot, and that night it would never have done at all.

'Not another murder?' exclaimed Sir Lancelot eagerly.

'Six,' returned McFiggie briefly.

'Good gracious me!' said Sir Lancelot.

'That's what I make the score at the moment. I'll have the devil's own job tomorrow sorting the bodies out. He'd cut the heads off, y'see,' McFiggie explained. 'The legs he stuck under the floorboards, and the arms were in the copper. He'd been boiling all day to get rid of 'em, and it was the stench that brought out the neighbours. Not that boiling works, o'course.' He gave another laugh. 'I can make up a skeleton from a few bits of bone, just like we've got left on our plates.'

'How absolutely intriguing,' breathed Sir Lancelot.

'And not only that –' The pathologist felt in his pocket. 'I can build a whole head from these, which we found in the cellar.' He rattled half-a-dozen objects on his bread plate. 'Teeth.'

The Bishop's wife screamed and pitched into the mashed potatoes.

'Oh, horror!' cried the Bishop.

'All right, all right!' Sir Lancelot jumped up. 'Don't get excited everybody, for Heaven's sake.'

'My wife! My poor wife!'

'Damn it, it's only a vasovagal attack.' He sounded as if it were a shocking breach of good table manners. 'And don't all crowd round the patient. Grimsdyke!'

'Sir?'

'Hand me that water jug.'

'Mercy, mercy!' muttered the Bishop, slapping his wife's hand.

'That won't do the slightest good,' Sir Lancelot told him, tipping the water over her. 'The best thing you can do is loosen her stays.'

'Had I better fetch the brandy from the next room, sir?' I was beginning to feel a bit concerned about all this.

'There's a good chap. Not the liqueur brandy, of course.'

By the time I'd found the right brandy and spent a few moments calming down the pretty Italian maid in the kitchen, the patient had been carted upstairs. The dining-room was empty except for McFiggie, who was staring absently at the table cloth, and Sir Lancelot, who had taken his seat again and was getting on with his dinner.

'I told Maud perfectly plainly earlier in the evening this room was far too stuffy,' he greeted me. 'Help yourself to some more turkey, my boy, before everything's stone cold.'

Personally, I thought the time had come to call it an evening. Shortly afterwards I collected McFiggie and put him in a passing taxi, feeling that my first social engagement with the Spratts hadn't been much of a success. And I'd hardly closed the front door before I could hear Lady Spratt starting up on her husband.

5

I parked the 1930 Bentley between Razzy's pair of Jaguars in the basement at Park Lane, and took the lift to his flat.

I must say, I felt pretty worried about Sir Lancelot. Admittedly, the pair of us had entertained our little differences in the past, particularly across the green baize tables in the examination hall. But it would be jolly unsporting not to respect him as both a great chap and a mighty surgeon, and anyway if it hadn't been for him I should have ended up weeks ago in McFiggie's filing cabinet. It struck me as a shocking pity that the end of his career should be dimmed through mixing himself up with Sexton Blake, and a frightful shame if he missed becoming President of the Royal College of Surgeons, particularly with all those free dinners they throw in.

But of course I soon stopped thinking about Sir Lancelot, or anything else at all except Ophelia, and got out of the lift doing little bits of mental arithmetic over the number of hours until I'd see her again. I felt for Razzy's key as I turned the corner of the corridor, and there the dear girl was, pummelling his doorbell.

'Ophelia!'

I bounded like a gazelle who'd trodden on an ant-hill.

'Darling, where on earth have you been?' she demanded. 'And all dressed up like that, too. I've been ringing this thing for simply hours.'

I was confused. 'But why aren't you still down in the country, helping your old people to finish up the cold turkey?'

'Something utterly sensational has happened –'

'Basil – ?'

My heart raced. Perhaps he'd been spotted by a horror-film producer and whisked off to Hollywood. Perhaps he'd eloped with the Fairy Queen. Perhaps he'd missed his cue for the trap door, and broken his blasted neck.

'No, it's Jeremy. He phoned me this morning with quite the most fabulous job in the world.'

'Jeremy? Jeremy who?'

I let her into the flat.

'Jeremy Graham. You know, he does the publicity for the Capricorn shipping people.'

'Ah, yes.'

I remembered a superior bird with tight trousers and a curly bowler we'd met in a pub.

'So I had to absolutely drop everything and fly. But here's the stupid thing.' Ophelia laughed. 'I've got to have a medical examination first. Me! Who's never had a day's illness in my life, and all my relatives living to be simply hundreds.'

'Medical examination?'

I wondered what on earth she was advertising, particularly as all the girls in the magazines seemed to be photographed in a state of advanced malnutrition.

'Yes, darling.' Ophelia made for the consulting-room. 'I'm going modelling on a ship. Isn't it thrilling? Three weeks all the way to South America, fly home, glorious sunshine, absolutely everything paid and no housework. What do I do now? Go behind that screen thing?'

'Now – now just a minute.'

She looked at me in surprise.

'What on earth's the matter, Gaston?'

'Nothing really, but ... well, this could be all most frightfully embarrassing.'

'Embarrassing?'

'I mean ... dash it! You ought really to go to some other doctor.'

'But darling! I don't *know* any other doctors.'

'Lots of them about,' I assured her. 'Reliable and courteous g.p.s on both sides of Sloane Street. Just stick a pin in a brass plate.'

'Gaston, you *are* making a fuss –'

'Professional etiquette, and all that –'

'Anyone would think I wanted you to cut my leg off, or something. After all, I've only come for a certificate.'

Ophelia disappeared behind the screen.

She left me wondering what to do. Naturally, in the profession one sees a fair slice of the population with its clothes off, and with no particular feelings except wondering how people ever become nudists unless suffering from advanced myopia. But I loved Ophelia. I'd put her on a ruddy great pedestal, like Queen Victoria outside Buckingham Palace. I was absolutely dashed if I was going behind that screen coldly to palpate the liver of the woman I adored, and ask all sorts of questions which would never have done in the drawing-room. And dressed in a dinner jacket, too.

'Do you want me to take everything off, darling?'

Bits of Ophelia's wardrobe not on public view began to flutter along the top of the screen.

'No, no, not everything! Only the essentials.'

'The essentials – ?'

'I mean, keep the essentials on. Really Ophelia!' I started to pace the peach-coloured carpet. 'This jolly well isn't fair.'

She seemed to find it rather funny.

'I do believe you're being coy, Gaston. And I thought you doctors were coldly indifferent to the human body?'

'Yes, but not to one you've taken out to dinner,' I told her smartly.

She laughed. 'I think I'm ready for you now, darling.'

I hesitated. Then I suddenly had one of those inspirations of mine, which often strike very profitably just as they're coming under starter's orders.

'I can't possibly examine you,' I exclaimed. 'Not this evening, at any rate.'

Ophelia's blonde head appeared.

'Don't tell me you have early closing, or something?'

'No. But I haven't got a chaperone.'

'A chaperone? Good God, man! What do I want a chaperone for? Or are you intending to send me home in a hansom?'

'Not for you, old girl,' I explained. 'But for me. Rule one in medical school – examine no female between the clavicles and the kneecap unless in the presence of another of her sex. And of course our receptionist is miles away at

this hour of the night. So you'll have to come back tomorrow morning.'

Ophelia drew a breath, sounding like an annoyed asp.

'I'm not at all certain, Dr Grimsdyke, that I entirely like
the tone of that remark.'

'Pure routine, of course,' I added quickly. Ophelia was a
delightfully high-spirited girl, but she did have a rather
hair-trigger temper and I didn't want to risk getting the
sphygmomanometer chucked at me.

'It's just that – well, otherwise we'd be committing the
most frightful professional misconduct,' I pointed out.

'Are you suggesting Dr Grimsdyke, that I have nothing
better to do with my evenings than going round London
compromising ham-fisted young medicos –'

'Nothing personal, I assure you –'

'Are you going to examine me or aren't you? Not only
must I have my certificate first thing tomorrow morning
but it's freezing cold behind here. If this is the way you
treat all your patients, I can only say you must be quite a
specialist in pneumonia.'

I went behind the screen.

A couple of minutes later found me at the Chippendale
consulting desk, writing a note on Razzy's paper to the
Capricorn Shipping Company of Leadenhall Street, saying
I had that day examined Miss Ophelia O'Brien (21), and
in my opinion she was suffering from no disabilities, physical
or mental.

'That was pretty short and sweet, I must say.' Ophelia's
voice seemed to have cheered up a good deal. 'Was my
chest all right?'

'Fine.'

'Dear Gaston!' She appeared round the screen. 'Are
you always so stern and severe with your female patients?'

'One has one's bedside manner,' I murmured. I felt it
high time for a little professional dignity.

She laughed. 'Be an angel and do up my bra for me.
The catch has gone.'

'Ophelia –' I began, obliging.

'Yes, darling?'

'Ophelia, old girl –'

What with the surprise of seeing her and the general confusion, I'd just realized the shocking blow about to fall on the Grimsdyke psychology.

'Why have you got to sail out of my life, just when we were getting along so jolly well together?' I demanded.

'But it's only for three weeks, darling. Anyone would think I was a sort of female Christopher Columbus, or something.'

'But in three weeks Basil will be back in Town!'

'Oh, yes. So he will.'

I shot her a glance as she reached for her stockings. If Ophelia didn't always take me seriously, it struck me she sometimes didn't take Basil with the gravity of the girl committed to darning his tights for the rest of her life.

'Don't you think it would be rather fun if we got married?' I mentioned.

'*Please*, Gaston, not again.' She fiddled with her suspenders. 'I thought we settled that old business the other night?'

That had been in a night-club, and you can't imagine how difficult it is convincing a girl your heart bleeds for her with everyone blowing squeakers and popping balloons all round you.

'Basil's a sterling chap, of course,' I conceded. 'Probably make a very good husband for someone one day. And admittedly the Grimsdyke prospects themselves aren't particularly bright. But,' I pointed out, 'if you married me instead, at least you'd get quicker delivery.'

Another thought struck me, as I noticed the coloured shipping brochure that had slipped from her handbag.

'You won't just forget poor old Uncle Grimsdyke, will you?' I asked, rather plaintive. 'Not on those romantic evenings in the tropical moonlight? Not when you're being waltzed round the deck by coves in white dinner jackets? Look, there's a picture of them here –'

'Surely a big grown man like you doesn't still believe in adverts?' Ophelia kissed me lightly on the left ear.

'No, but –'

'Besides, it's probably the monsoon season in South America, anyway, with all the nights pitch black and everyone being seasick.'

She wiggled into her slip.

'I know!' she exclaimed. 'Why don't you come too? Then we can have lovely fun, with the shuffle-board and the ping-pong and the swims before breakfast.'

I gave a sigh. 'Absolutely ruddy impossible, I'm afraid. In the present state of my finances, I could hardly raise the bus fare to the docks.'

'Of course, you'd have to pay, darling, wouldn't you? I was quite forgetting. Now I must rush – be a sweet and zip up my dress – I've got simply loads of things to do in my flat if I'm off on Monday week.'

'Ophelia –' I grabbed her hand. 'Surely I can at least take you out a bit before you go?'

'But I'll be frantically busy, with shopping and choosing clothes and hair-do's and everything.'

'How about tomorrow evening?'

'I've got a special session with Jeremy.'

'Tomorrow afternoon, then?'

'But darling! On Sunday afternoon London's as dead as Pompeii.'

'Please, Ophelia –'

'Oh, all right.' She adjusted her make-up. 'We can go and have a nice cup of tea somewhere, can't we? Thank you so much for the certificate.'

She kissed the other ear.

'You're an absolutely divine doctor,' she ended, gathering up her bag, 'and I can hardly wait to be properly ill and send for you to hold my hand and do all those clever things over again.'

She left.

The Grimsdyke life was in ruins. I would never again have the chance of seeing the dear girl without that blasted fellow Basil prowling in the background. I gave a ruddy great sigh. On the whole, I'd had a pretty miserable evening. I wondered if it would be particularly chilly simply ending it all from Westminster Bridge. But I decided against it, and took off my tie and went to bed instead. Though I thought it would have jolly well served McFiggie right, being called to St Swithin's in the morning with a shocking hangover and finding I'd got there already.

6

I grabbed Razzy's pink bedside telephone as it rang at seven-thirty in the morning.

'Hello, angel face –'

'Grimsdyke? Spratt here.'

'Oh good, morning, sir. Thank you for a very charming dinner –'

'Anything likely to keep you in your practice this afternoon?'

I thought quickly, for that hour of the morning.

'I've a couple of routine diabetics to see –'

'Presumably they can wait until the evening. I wish you to accompany me to the Zoo.'

'The Zoo, sir?'

'You heard perfectly well what I said.'

The old boy struck me as rather bad-tempered.

'Owing to her performance yesterday the Bishop's lady professes herself too ill to take her children, who have been screaming their blasted heads off all night at the prospect of being disappointed. The Bishop apparently can't be seen in public anywhere on Sundays. Or so he tells me. My wife therefore thinks that I should play the nursemaid.'

I supposed that morning even Sir Lancelot hadn't the courage to refuse.

'I would much appreciate it if you would come to give me moral support, Grimsdyke.'

'As a matter of fact, sir,' I hedged, 'it might all be rather difficult –'

'Kindly be at my house at two o'clock sharp,' said Sir Lancelot, and rang off.

This didn't leave much alternative to telephoning Ophelia about eleven and scrubbing the tea. She didn't seem broken hearted. In fact, she giggled a good bit and made a rather rude joke about the baboons. Then it started pouring with rain and the wind turned raw enough to give the penguins frostbite, so on the whole it was a pretty miserable Grimsdyke who drove down Oxford Street again that afternoon.

Sir Lancelot was already at the front door, dressed in a knickerbocker suit and a deerstalker hat, which I supposed he thought the correct costume for visiting Zoos.

'I was wondering if you were going to funk the whole outing,' he greeted me. 'I shouldn't have blamed you. I only wish I had the nerve to do so myself. Now I suppose "If it were done when 'tis done, then 'twere well it were done quickly". I shall summon the brats.'

A few minutes later I was able to make a closer inspection of the Bishop's two youngest.

Hilda was a pale thin girl suffering from crooked eyes and crooked teeth, both of which were undergoing rather ostentatious clinical correction. Randoph was short and dark, with a nasty scowl and a general air of wanting to go and blow something up. I was rather at a loss to open the conversation, because I'm never at my best with children. I don't think Sir Lancelot was either, but he always solved the problem simply by refusing to admit they existed, and treating anyone past the age of weaning just like another adult.

'You children will kindly jump into the back of my car and we can get started,' he commanded. 'If either of you feels the slightest inclination to vomit you are to inform me at once.'

'So kind of you to take them, my dear Lancelot.' The Bishop appeared in the doorway. 'My poor wife is still far from herself. It is turning into some form of migraine, I fear. Most distressing. But it would be such a shame to disappoint the little darlings, wouldn't it? Now if you'll excuse me, I shall get back to the fire. The weather is extremely treacherous these winter days, don't you think?'

We left, Sir Lancelot slamming all the car doors in turn.

'How I am to bring myself to spend three whole weeks under the same roof as that feller without developing acute paranoid schizophrenia is totally beyond my comprehension,' he exploded, pressing a button to put the children out of earshot behind the glass partition of his Rolls. 'Not content with his wife making a first-class exhibition of herself in front of my guests yesterday evening, he ruins my breakfast this morning by describing minutely all his symptoms during the night. "I never closed my eyes for a second", he said. And I could hear him snoring his head off till the milk arrived.'

'I suppose even clerics are a bit easy with the Ninth Commandment when it comes to telling their doctors how little they sleep,' I suggested.

The surgeon snorted. 'I don't want so much as a word about him in my biography, understand? My own family is bad enough, but Maud's is the ruddy limit.'

He blew the horn as he narrowly missed turning a cyclist into an orthopaedic case in the middle of the Marylebone Road.

'Perhaps I should have informed you about my relations a little more fully,' Sir Lancelot continued in a calmer voice, as we nosed into Regent's Park. 'I am one of five brothers, none of whom has been on speaking terms since the measles. Two I should prefer not to mention. Of the others, my youngest brother George ran away to sea at an early age after a misunderstanding with the Vicar over the choir funds. Though I am glad to say he has subsequently redeemed himself to some measure by becoming – Damnation! It's starting to snow.'

'Perhaps we should put it off till next week?' I suggested. There was still time to hold Ophelia's hand over the tea-cakes.

'Certainly not. I refuse to have next Sunday utterly ruined as well. Now come along you children,' commanded Sir Lancelot, lowering the partition as we drew up before the Zoo gates. 'Button your coats and blow your noses and we'll be off.'

We stepped out of the car.

The snow was settling on Sir Lancelot's Ulster and started to run down my neck in that nasty mocking way it has. It had just struck me that nobody else could possibly be so idiotic to visit the Zoo on an afternoon like that, when I noticed a chap waiting by the turnstile. He was a small, seedy-looking fellow in an old macintosh and a bowler, with a floppy moustache and gold-rimmed glasses and carrying an attaché case. Just as we formed up behind him I was a bit startled to see him give a little jump and start retreating backwards down the pavement.

'After you, my dear sir, after you,' boomed Sir Lancelot.

The little man hesitated a moment, then chucked some silver at the gateman and clicked rapidly inside.

'We seemed to have rather staggered the other visitor,' I remarked, as we followed.

'And can't you believe it?' replied Sir Lancelot shortly. 'Now, you two – what do you want to look at first? Eh? Damnation! Didn't you go before you left home? Grimsdyke!'

'Sir?'

'You take charge of that side of the operations. As both these infants seem to be suffering from congenital hypoplasia of the bladder, I shall attempt to seek refuge from the elements in that kiosk until their symptoms are relieved.'

When we got back Sir Lancelot was shivering, and Randolph announced he wanted a ride on an elephant.

'I doubt very much if you'll find an elephant plying for hire this afternoon,' his uncle told him loftily. 'I am afraid you will have to content yourself with merely observing one of the creatures through the – in the name of heaven, Grimsdyke! Can't you control him?'

The little horror let out a scream and started pummelling Sir Lancelot's legs with his fists.

'You, girl!' he roared. 'Don't just stand there. You're his big sister. Try and shut him up.'

Hilda pouted. 'He's been promised a ride on an elephant since his birthday.'

'You can't expect me to produce elephants out of a hat, you ugly little moron.'

'I'll tell my Mummy you called me that.'

'All right, all right! I'll see if I can find a ruddy elephant. In heaven's name, detach this child from my overcoat.'

I obliged, by exerting surgical traction on his ear.

'Now let us go and look at the monkeys.'

'I don't want to see any monkeys,' announced the girl. 'I want an ice-cream.'

'Good God!' Sir Lancelot wiped the snow from his face. 'Ice cream!'

I had the bright idea of settling for a few bars of chocolate, and slipped all my loose change into a convenient slot-machine. This shut up the brats until we reached the monkey-house, which at least was nice and warm. But you know what monkeys are. The way they were carrying on even Sir Lancelot felt the children should be moved, and as they were both laughing their heads off I fancied we might have another scene. But fortunately Sir Lancelot could be a pretty crafty opponent, even for that pair.

'Let us now,' he announced mysteriously. 'Go and visit the *Equus caballus*.'

From the way the kids started jumping up and down I suppose they expected some fabulous monster, probably with two heads. They looked pretty disappointed when faced with just a couple of ordinary ponies.

'The evolution of the horse,' began Sir Lancelot, before they had time to complain, 'which developed from a small four-toed Eocene mammal, is both interesting and instructive.'

He then gave a short zoological lecture stuffed with Latin, which silenced them completely.

Sir Lancelot had only got as far as the *Mesohippus* when an odd movement caught my eye at the end of the pony house. It was the little chap in the bowler peeping at us round the corner.

'Feller's probably mad,' grunted the surgeon when I mentioned this. 'Though it's a strange thing, Grimsdyke – I could swear I've seen him somewhere before.'

'Probably one of your patients, sir?'

He shook his head. 'I never forget an abdomen or a face. However, we have more than madmen to worry about. Now, you two children, we shall go and inspect the *Mus Rattus*.'

As we struggled down the Elephant Walk in driving snow towards the rodent house, I was a bit surprised to hear Sir Lancelot give a laugh.

'Talking of faces, I've just remembered who the hairy baboon reminds me of. My brother George – the one who ran away to sea.'

The snow down my neck had reached my twelfth thoracic vertebra, so I could only rise to a polite murmur about imagining it on the bridge with a peaked cap and a telescope in a hurricane.

'I can assure you my brother George has not suffered the slightest discomfort from the elements for years, except when he has forgotten his umbrella. He has an extremely agreeable office in the City, where he has risen to be Marine Superintendent of the Capricorn Shipping Line.'

I gave a start.

'The Capricorn Line, sir?'

But before I could say any more Sir Lancelot gripped my arm.

'Look at that! The feller in the bowler again.'

He was wiping snow from one of those big plans of the Zoo they put up here and there. With a little shriek, he shot out of sight behind the aviary.

'I told you he was insane,' snorted Sir Lancelot.

'He certainly seems to be behaving rather oddly.'

'So are we, being here at all in this weather. Now children, here is our next exhibit.'

'What a swizz,' complained Hilda, 'they're only rats.'

'I assure you, young lady, that the dental structure of the rat is utterly fascinating.'

'I want to see the lions,' grumbled Randolph.

'*Panthera leo* by all means. I believe they are kept over here.'

We pitched into the snow again. We were all four soaked to the skin, but I myself was glowing inside like a blast furnace. I'd had a terrific idea about Sir Lancelot's brother, and I was just wondering how to work it out when there was that damn little man again, nipping round the antelopes and shooting into the lion house.

'Grimsdyke!'

Sir Lancelot stopped.

'Sir?'

'I'm inclined to think there is more in this bowler-hatted feller than meets the eye.'

'He may simply be rather fond of animals, sir?'

'H'm. We shall nevertheless investigate. Now you two children.' He glared at them. 'Keep close behind me, and if you make so much as a squeak I'll chuck you in the bear pit.'

We crept through the snow to the door of the lion house. We peeped inside. There was the little man with his attaché case open, throwing chunks of meat to a bunch of highly appreciative carnivores behind the bars.

'By George!' Sir Lancelot hissed in my ear. 'Now I know who the feller reminds me of. Crippen!'

'What, Crippen the murderer, sir?'

'Of course Crippen the murderer! He's exactly the same type – meek little man in a stiff collar and glasses, and as dangerous as hell. Good God, Grimsdyke! We're witnessing the crime of the century.'

I didn't quite follow all this.

'Don't be dense, boy! You chop up your wife, and what do you do with her? Why – feed her to the lions in the Zoo, of course!'

'But he may just be having a bit of fun, like people with monkey-nuts –'

'Hi, there! You!'

I was a bit alarmed as Sir Lancelot strode into the lion house.

'Here, I say!' I exclaimed. 'Hold on, sir –'

I was even more alarmed when the Crippen chap gave a yell, chucked the last of the meat through the bars, and made for the far door with the senior surgeon of St Swithin's in pursuit.

'Stop that man!' shouted Sir Lancelot. 'Stop him, I say!'

I stood in the snow. I wondered what to do. Sir Lancelot chased the chap round the penguins, while the children jumped up and down in delight. They hadn't had such fun since a visiting curate got caught in the motor-mower.

The little man dived for one of those revolving iron exit gates, with Sir Lancelot close behind. I grabbed the children's chocolate-plastered gloves and followed. I must say, I felt pretty worried. Sir Lancelot was making an absolutely first class ruddy fool of himself. Distinguished surgical gents simply can't go round London chasing tender-hearted little men who feel the lions need a bit of fattening up. And when I got the brats outside, there was Sir Lancelot holding his quarry by the macintosh collar, and probably committing all sorts of actionable assault.

'All right, guv'nor,' the little man kept repeating. 'I'll come quiet. It's a fair cop all right, and I shouldn't never have done it.'

'Good Lord!' I exclaimed, a bit horrified. 'Then he really is a –'

'Fetch a constable,' commanded Sir Lancelot. 'Careful what you say, you villain. Any statement you make I shall reduce to writing and produce in evidence at your trial.'

'Oh, Gawd!'

I found a policeman. He looked about sixteen, and approached with a sort of air I'd worn myself when nabbed by Sister for an awkward case in Casualty.

'Officer, take this man in charge. A very serious crime has been committed.'

The little man cried, 'I confess everything,' and burst into tears. The children gave another roar of laughter. Their uncle had finally come up to scratch on the afternoon's entertainment.

'Name and address, please, sir,' said the policeman, reaching for his notebook.

'My dear good man! Don't stand there taking names and addresses as though he'd parked on the wrong side of the street. I tell you that something of the utmost seriousness has been committed. Do you know who I am? I am a surgeon. Indeed, I am the consultant surgeon to the Police Welfare Club, and I demand to be taken to your superior officers immediately. Ah, a police car! I am glad somebody had the intelligence to reach for the telephone. Grimsdyke!'

'Sir?'

'You will kindly take the children home in my Rolls. The scene is far too painful for their eyes.'

'What's going on here?' called a policeman from the car.

'Let us all go to the nearest police station and find out,' said Sir Lancelot.

7

Our return minus Sir Lancelot caused quite a stir in Harley Street.

'Not an accident!' exclaimed the Bishop, I fancied a shade too hopefully.

'No, not an accident,' I assured him, while everyone seemed to be talking at once. 'But it is rather complicated –'

'Oh, dear,' exclaimed Lady Spratt.

'You see, the police –'

'The police?' murmured the Bishop. 'Horror!'

'And I'd better not discuss it in front of the children –'

'Mummy,' said Hilda, 'Sir Lancelot called me an ugly little moron.'

The brats were smartly removed by the Bishop's eldest daughter, and I led the others into the drawing-room.

'We had a rather odd experience,' I started. I shifted a bit, what with everyone staring at me. 'Fact is, we witnessed the aftermath of a murder.'

'Murder!' gasped the Bishop.

'Lancelot wasn't involved –?' cried Lady Spratt.

'Only in nabbing the criminal,' I reassured her quickly.

'It is really most unfortunate that we should become mixed up in such matters,' remarked the Bishop's wife.

'But Gaston, what on earth happened?' demanded Lady Spratt.

'We were all in the lion house.' It really was dashed difficult knowing exactly how to put it. 'And there was the murderer chap, tossing great chunks of meat through the bars from his suitcase. You see, we were actually watching him disposing of the body.'

The Bishop's wife gave a scream, and fainted again.

'Horror upon horror!' cried the Bishop.

There was naturally a good deal of confusion, even though

we'd already established the drill for this situation. But what with carting his wife to the sofa and the smelling salts and the brandy and the Bishop fanning her with his apron, I couldn't get any further with the story before Sir Lancelot appeared himself in a police car, looking pleased with life.

'Lancelot! What on earth have you been up to?' insisted Lady Spratt at once.

'Furthering the ends of justice, my dear. Where are our guests?'

'Charles is just upstairs helping his wife. She was taken ill again.'

'Really? Something's constitutionally wrong with that woman. It might not be a bad idea if I had a look at her. There you are, Grimsdyke. You'll stay for tea?'

'Tea!' Lady Spratt started to get cross. 'How you have the nerve to talk about tea when we are all of us in a state of utter emotional exhaustion –'

'You really must try and keep calm, my dear. Once I get this beastly wet overcoat off I shall give you the full story. Meanwhile, I see no reason whatever why I should forgo my usual tea.'

And a pretty dramatic story it was, too.

When Sir Lancelot had arrived at the police station, where he was lucky to find he'd once repaired the sergeant's hernia, the little man was incapable of anything except loud sobs.

'Aware that vital evidence was rapidly disappearing in the gastric juices of lions,' Sir Lancelot explained, as the pretty little Italian maid wheeled in the tea-trolley, 'I immediately directed the police to telephone McFiggie. McFiggie naturally grasped the point at once, and agreed that the animals should have an emetic, which has already been administered. Once the stomach contents are under his microscope he will be able to tell if there is any trace of human flesh remaining undigested. Elementary, my dear Grimsdyke.'

He then settled down to his usual Sunday spread of hot buttered crumpets and dundee cake.

Fact is, I fancied Lady Spratt now felt as proud of the old boy as I did myself. For all that chasing round the penguins, the quick-wittedness which had pulled off so many tricky surgical diagnoses in the wards at St Swithin's had copped the perpetrator of a particularly crafty and messy murder. It just proved again how Sir Lancelot made a resounding success of anything he happened to take an interest in, from surgery to snipe-shooting and collecting rare diseases to collecting rare china.

'Lancelot, how provident to see you safe and sound.' The Bishop appeared in the doorway, looking flustered. 'I fear that my wife –'

'My dear feller, take a seat. I have a most interesting story to tell.'

'My poor wife ... not very well.'

'Indeed? I'm extremely sorry to hear it.'

'Thank you, thank you. The London air.... I don't think it quite suits her. It would perhaps be for the best if we all shortly returned home again.'

'Very wise of you,' agreed Sir Lancelot, swallowing half a crumpet. 'As for my adventures today, you can read all about them in the morning papers.'

'Papers!' The Bishop went pale. 'If you wouldn't mind ... no abuse of your kind hospitality ... we shall be on our way quite early tomorrow.'

'I'll give instructions for Maria to call you at six.' Sir Lancelot glanced through the window. 'Ah, the police again. My former patient, Sergeant Griffin, I see.'

The Bishop stared at the black saloon outside.

'Perhaps, Lancelot, if it wouldn't seem impolite, we had better leave tonight. The traffic on the roads tomorrow, you understand –'

'Then I shall give Maria instructions to help you with the packing straight away. Come in, Sergeant, come in.' The Bishop bumped into the policeman in his hurry to be out of sight. 'Cup of tea? Cigarette?'

'No thank you, Sir Lancelot. Good afternoon, madam. Good afternoon, sir,' the Sergeant added to me. He put his helmet on a handy occasional table. 'Well, Sir Lancelot,' he began, 'you've done a fine job of work for us, and no mistake.'

'I am always delighted to be of assistance to the police,' declared the surgeon, munching a slice of cake.

'We've been after that chap for quite a time.'

'Good heavens! You mean he's committed a number of murders?'

The sergeant smiled. 'Very droll of you to put it like that, sir. I suppose he did murder the poor things.'

'No two ways about it, I should think,' remarked Lady Spratt sharply.

'We've got the report from Dr McFiggie, and the C.I.D. have searched the fellow's premises up at Crouch End. Quite a bit of evidence they found there. He'd have made a good many visits to the Zoo before he finished the job. Could have cost him a small fortune in admission fees in the end.'

'You couldn't possibly get a whole body in an attaché case,' Sir Lancelot agreed.

'There were a good many bodies. His refrigerator was packed with them.'

'Ugh!' cried Lady Spratt. I must admit a shiver went up and down my own spine.

'How dastardly!' exclaimed Sir Lancelot.

'I agree, sir. I fancy the R.S.P.C.A. will have charges to bring as well.'

Sir Lancelot stared. 'The R.S.P.C. what?'

'The Royal Society for the Prevention of Cruelty to Animals –'

'Yes, yes! I know, I know –'

'Some of them poor things must have been killed very carelessly.'

Sir Lancelot rose.

'One moment, Sergeant. You will kindly explain yourself?'

The policeman looked surprised. . .

'Doesn't seem much to explain, sir. I've got Dr McFiggie's phone message here.' He pulled a scrap of paper from his tunic pocket. 'It says, "Microscopical examination of stomach contents from lions A, B, and C shows large masses of undigested muscular tissue, probably originating from cat or dog". The fellow you caught runs a small pork-pie business,' he explained. 'We've suspected for months he was putting bits of stray dogs and cats in his stuff, and once he got wind we were on his trail he tried to get rid of the evidence.

Ah, well – crime doesn't pay in the end, sir, does it?'

There was a silence.

'No,' said Sir Lancelot shortly. 'It doesn't.'

'Sergeant, are you *sure* you won't have a cup of tea?' asked Lady Spratt.

A few minutes later I was alone with Sir Lancelot in his study.

'Grimsdyke –'

'Sir?'

'Grimsdyke, you will not utter a word of the true story of this afternoon.'

'Wouldn't dream of it, sir.'

'I think I can silence that legalized Burke and Hare, McFiggie. I never did like the feller much, anyway. I shall have to resign from the Police Welfare Club, of course. But that was an intolerable waste of time. For the rest, I must rely on your discretion, or I shall be unable to take luncheon in the hospital refectory again if there happens to be steak pie on the menu.'

'Believe me, sir, I'd do anything for you,' I told him stoutly.

'Thank you, Grimsdyke. You are a damned chatterbox, but this time I believe you. And – and I sincerely appreciate it,' he added quickly. Sir Lancelot paused. 'If there is anything I might do in return ...?'

'Do you think you could give me an introduction to your brother, sir?' I asked at once. 'The sailor chap? I was thinking of taking a little paid holiday while getting on with your memoirs.'

'Ship's doctor, you mean? Assuredly I shall give you a reference.' He sat at the desk. 'Just tell me what to write. From long experience on appointment boards I know that no testimonial is the slightest use unless written by the applicant.'

'That's jolly decent of you, sir,'

'I am more than happy to be of assistance.' Sir Lancelot took the cap off his fountain pen. He paused, and gave a smile. 'And there's one thing, my boy. At least I managed to get rid of the blasted Bishop.'

8

'Enter!'

It was the next morning, and that voice was chillingly familiar.

'Yes?'

'Er – Dr Grimsdyke, sir. They just sent in a letter about me.'

'Sit.'

Captain George Spratt, wearing a plain blue serge suit in an office filled with rather pleasant models of ships, took a silver box from his pocket and whisked a pile of black snuff into each nostril.

'So you want a voyage, eh?'

'That was the general idea, sir.'

He sat glaring at me for half a minute. I'd always felt that Sir Lancelot himself wouldn't have looked out of place pacing the poop of the *Bounty*, but his brother George resembled Blackbeard the Pirate after a heavy night on the rum trying to decide whether to flay the captives alive or have them boiled slowly in oil.

'Very convenient for you medical gentlemen, isn't it?' he began, as though hailing something through fog. 'Walking about with a built-in steamship ticket? Eh? Though my brother seems to write very highly of you.' The Captain paused. 'I don't suppose he mentions me much, does he?'

As a matter of fact, Sir Lancelot did keep pretty quiet about his brother George, but I tried to indicate in a few words that he was always being held up as embodying the best nautical qualities of Sir Francis Drake and Grace Darling.

'He told you that scurrilous tale about the choir funds, I suppose? Totally untrue, of course. Years afterwards they found out that the Vicar had boozed the lot.' Captain

Spratt tossed Sir Lancelot's letter aside. 'You want to sail on Monday in the *Capricorn Queen*?'

'I'd very much like that particular ship, sir.'

I tried not to slip off the chair in eagerness.

'Well, I suppose Dr O'Rory has been pestering me long enough for a voyage off.' The Captain sat stroking his beard. 'Needs it too, from the reports I've been getting. Now look here young feller me lad – going to sea doesn't mean an extended bout of skylarking at the Company's expense. Understand? Doctors are members of our crews, and expected to comport themselves as such. If you want to drink yourself to death, you can do that with less trouble to everybody ashore. As for women, the only time you hold a lady's hand at sea is to give up your place in the lifeboat as the ship goes down. Get that straight to start with.'

'Yes, sir.'

I must say, I was glad that Captain Spratt was as landlocked as Sir Joseph Porter, K.C.B., the Ruler of the Queen's Navee. Even for dear Ophelia I wouldn't be shut up with a chap like him for six weeks in a floating steel strong-box.

'Though God knows why anyone at all wants to go to sea today.' The Captain treated his nose to another meal of snuff. 'You look a man of the world, Doctor,' he conceded. 'Know anything about advertising agencies?'

'Advertising agencies, sir?'

'Your best friend wouldn't tell you, and all that rubbish. Anyone would imagine the entire human race stank like a herd of goats. We've got some hag from one of them sailing this trip, to be photographed in her bathing drawers all over the deck. I'm only warning you.'

'Thank you, sir.'

'The Company's gone raving mad about advertising.' He banged the desk so hard all the ships quivered. 'Even had a snapshot taken of *me*, God help them! By some ghastly wallahs in pink trousers who kept calling each other dearie.'

'I – I hope it came out nicely, sir.'

'When *I* first took command, passengers came aboard to travel, not to participate in some sort of floating Babylonian orgy. Hell's teeth! In those days you could maintain order and discipline aboard – silence in the afternoons and everyone up for breakfast, and so on. If passengers wanted amusement, there was always bingo on Saturday nights. You are fond of bingo, Doctor?'

'I don't think I've played, sir.'

'Anyway, they've changed bingo to Thursdays. On Saturdays my unfortunate Captains are obliged to put on paper hats and dance the rumba with a bunch of old ladies who'd be far better tucked up with a hot water bottle in Bournemouth. Nobody at sea knows where they are any more. At this rate we'll be moving Divine Service to Wednesday afternoons. When can you join?'

'Join? You mean it's – it's all fixed? Absolutely any time you like, sir.'

Razzy had shown up with his sprained ankles and sun blisters, the husband had gone back to the Himalayas and taken the actress with him, so I was professionally on the loose again.

'Report on board eight o'clock Friday morning to check medical stores,' ordered Captain Spratt briefly. 'You will now step next door to be introduced to Captain Makepeace, who is in command of your vessel.' He held out his hand. 'It only remains for me to wish you a pleasant voyage, Doctor. We shall meet again on your return to port.'

I was pretty relieved to discover Captain Makepeace a little thin chap with a bowler and umbrella beside him, sitting at a desk signing some papers.

'You may have found Captain Spratt somewhat direct in his manner,' he began mildly, as we were left alone.

'Bluff old sea-dog, and all that,' I remarked.

'Pray do not be discomforted by him, Doctor. I was his Chief Officer for some years, and I fear I let it undermine my health.' Captain Makepeace laid a hand on his right hip pocket. 'The kidneys, you know. I still suffer from the twinges. Perhaps you could suggest something –?'

'Delighted to give you a thorough going-over once I'm aboard,' I said quickly, it being clearly important to keep in with the chap.

'Thank you, Doctor. I should be most obliged. It is indeed a great relief to have an enthusiastic young medical man like yourself with us. A great relief. Dr O'Rory, I fear, has been behaving very oddly of late. Of course, he has been at sea for many years.'

I nodded. It is well known in the profession that prolonged service afloat induces certain irreversible psychological changes.

'He became very interested in the Great Pyramid – all the measurements, you understand. Unless he consulted them he was unable to decide anything at all, from the day to get his hair cut to the prescription for some unfortunate person appearing in his surgery.'

Captain Makepeace gave a faint smile.

'Of course, I am not so strict at sea as Captain Spratt would suggest. We live in modern times, Doctor. Indeed, I rather encourage my officers to drink with the passengers.'

'Excellent social move, sir.'

'And to pay some little attentions to the unaccompanied young ladies.'

I nodded. 'The poor things might get frightfully lonely otherwise.'

'We must make our own fun at sea, you know. Do you like bingo, Doctor? If you wish, you can call out the numbers. Dr O'Rory did, and very witty he was too, until recently he started getting a bit near the knuckle for the ladies.' We shook hands. 'I am sure, Doctor, our next voyage will be a particularly happy one.'

'I'm absolutely positive,' I agreed warmly.

Thus I appeared up the gangway of the *Capricorn Queen* before breakfast the following Friday morning, dressed up in as much gold braid as the chap who hails the taxis outside Fortnum's.

The *Capricorn Queen* was a great white thing like a wedding cake with portholes, though as she was tied to Tilbury Docks I'd nothing much to do for the week-end, except sit on the sofa that ran down one side of my cabin like the seat in a second-class railway compartment, smoking duty-free cigarettes and reading *Lord Hornblower*.

I hadn't said a word to Ophelia about my being aboard, because I thought it would come as a nice surprise. Besides she might have decided to stay at home once she realized we were leaving old Basil on the beach at Blackport. I was, of course, being a simply frightful cad, nipping up the gangway behind the poor chap's back. But the thought of all that tropical moonlight in store not only shoved the thought into my subconscious, but fairly made me want to go skipping round the deck.

I spent an impatient few days until they put a match to the boilers, and with a good deal of confusion we edged round to Tilbury landing stage, where passengers are let on by those chaps who handle passports as though they were Christmas cards from the Isolation Hospital. You can imagine I was pretty well jumping with excitement, particularly when I fancied I spotted Ophelia's legs disappearing up a companion-way. I'd asked the Chief Steward to put a whacking great bunch of roses in her cabin with a little note simply inviting her to cocktails at six with the ship's doctor, and I could hardly wait to see her face as she opened my cabin door and saw me waiting to mix her first Martini.

In no time we were on our way to South America, which to start with runs between Plumstead Marshes and Barking Creek. I changed into a clean white collar and polished up my brass buttons. Six o'clock arrived. I sat on the edge of the sofa and wondered exactly what Ophelia would say.

As it happened, she jolly near fainted.

'Gaston!' She gave a shriek. 'What in heaven's name are *you* doing here?'

I bowed and kissed her hand.

'Your humble shipmate.'

'But you aren't a sailor!'

'Yes I am,' I corrected her. 'At the moment, just as much as Nelson or old Father Noah himself. I'm the official ship's doctor.'

She stared at me.

'But – but for God's sake *why*?'

'Ophelia my sweet,' I explained simply. 'For you.'

'For me? What on earth do you mean, for me? How can you possibly –'

I kissed her hand again.

'For you,' I repeated, 'have I adopted the rough and uncertain calling of a seafarer –'

'You must be crazy!'

'No, no, Ophelia!' I started edging her towards the sofa. 'It's not crazy at all. Just think, for three blissful weeks you and I will be absolutely alone – apart from the other passengers of course.'

I had another go at her hand.

'By then, my dear old girl,' I went on, warming a bit, 'in the intimacy of shipboard life you will have grown to know me better. You may perhaps have grown to know me well enough to understand the terrible yearning –'

'Where are the cigarettes, darling?' asked Ophelia recovering herself.

'Oh, sorry. Over here.'

She sat down on the sofa.

'I wish you'd sent me a postcard or something first, darling.'

'But I wanted it to be a nice surprise.'

'It was certainly all of that,' she agreed.

I offered the duty-free cigarette tin.

'I hope you liked the flowers I sent to your cabin?'

'Which ones were they, darling? The ship's like a floating Kew Gardens.'

'Ophelia –' I flicked my lighter.

'Yes, darling?'

'Ophelia, I . . . I hope you don't mind my coming along for the ride?'

'I don't mind what you do, Gaston. If you want to go about dressed like a bus conductor, that's your affair.'

That was a bit irking. I'd hoped to cut a modest dash, what with all those brass buttons.

'But Ophelia!' I protested. 'You yourself said what terrific fun it would be if only I could make the trip.'

'Did I, darling?'

'Of course you did. With the early morning dips and the ping pong and the shuffle-board. Surely you remember?'

'A pretty palatial cabin you've got here, I must say,' observed Ophelia, blowing out a cloud of smoke.

'Not bad, is it? Nice and handy for the first-class swimming pool and the Veranda Bar.'

'The stinking little slot they've given me down below isn't big enough to swing the ship's cat in.'

I patted her hand. 'I'll get it changed,' I told her. 'Pretty important chap on board, the ship's doctor, you know. In fact, anything you should happen to want during the voyage –' I edged a bit up the sofa. 'Anything at all, you've only got to ask old Uncle Grimsdyke, who is ever at your devoted –'

'What's the other door with the red cross on it?'

'That? That's the hospital.'

'What an extraordinary thing to have on a ship! May I see?'

'Of course,' I replied politely, though preferring to continue the conversation on the sofa. 'All very neatly arranged, don't you think?' I added, opening the door.

'What's that heap of old iron doing in the corner?'

'That's the fully collapsible operating table.'

'How gruesome!'

'Oh yes, you can have your stomach out on board if you want to,' I explained. 'The Company spares no expense over the passengers' amenities.'

Ophelia gave a shiver.

'I *was* invited here for a drink, wasn't I?'

'I say, I'm frightfully sorry. All the stewards are at sixes and sevens stowing away the passengers, and my chap hasn't shown up yet. I'll give the fellow a buzz.'

'What on earth are these? Nut crackers for coconuts?'

'They're obstetrical forceps.'

'What awful things you have round you! I'd no idea you were that sort of doctor at all.'

Ophelia then got interested in the amputation set, so I left her fiddling with the muscle scalpel and rang the bell in my cabin.

'Ah, Steward,' I said, re-arranging the cushions to make the sofa nice and comfy for her. 'I'd like you to put out the gin from my spirit locker, and just nip across to the Veranda Bar and collect a pitcher of ice with half-a-dozen tonics and – Good God!' I cried. 'You!'

'Good God!' exclaimed Basil Beauchamp. 'You!'

9

I slammed the hospital door. Basil and I stood staring at each other like a couple of lobsters caught in the same pot.

'What the devil are you doing here?' I demanded. 'Dressed up like that?'

'Exactly the same, dear chappie,' he replied very affably, 'might I ask you.'

'But I'm the ship's doctor!'

'And I'm the ship's steward. Or at least, one of them. There's a good dozen sharing my cabin down below for a start. Still, that's nothing after provincial dressing-rooms. But my dear Grim! What a delightful surprise to meet you. And what an amazing coincidence. How's the cut of my white jacket? I picked it up yesterday from the theatrical costumier's.'

I grabbed the hospital door handle.

'I – I've got a difficult patient in here,' I said quickly. 'Hysterical female, you know.'

'How terribly exciting for you.'

'Just give me a moment to get rid of her.'

'But of course.'

'And we'll settle down to a nice cosy chat.'

I slipped inside the hospital.

'Darling,' said Ophelia, 'you don't use these saw things on *people*, surely?'

I seized her arm. 'Terribly sorry, old girl. An awkward patient's just turned up in my cabin –'

'Well, I must say! I was asked here for a quiet drink –'

'The doctor's life, you understand.' I gave a little laugh. 'Professional duties first, never know what's going to turn up next, and all that. No, no! Not that door.'

She looked startled.

'My patient's frightfully infective. Never do to mix with

him. Probably smallpox. The other door here leads straight on deck. Know your way back to your cabin? Mind the step. Bye-bye . . .'

Ophelia disappeared, rather mystified. I staggered back through the hospital. Reaching my own cabin, I found Basil with his feet up on my sofa, pouring himself a glass of my gin.

'But this is perfectly astounding, dear chappie!' He helped himself to one of my cigarettes. 'How on earth did you come to be aboard?'

'I wanted a holiday. Run down, you know. Overwork in Town. The sea air should do me a world of good.'

'Yes, you do look a bit hot and flushed,' Basil sniffed. 'That's very odd.'

'What's very odd?' I asked shortly.

'That smell. It's like the perfume my fiancée uses.'

'It's the antiseptic. But what about you?' I demanded, coming to the point. 'Surely at this very moment you should be amusing the little kiddies up at Blackport?'

'So I should, dear chappie, so I should. But the good burghers of Blackport, given ample opportunity and invitation to witness our little entertainment, refused to avail themselves of the chance. When the cast started outnumbering the audience the management felt they had inflicted sufficient suffering on both sides of the footlights, and put up the notice.'

'What a damned nuisance! I mean, what a damn shame.'

'On the contrary, it was absolutely a blessing in disguise. Blackport was a ghastly place, anyway, all tripe and trams.' Basil unhooked the collar of his jacket. 'But do I hear you ask,' he continued amiably, 'why I should exchange the freedom of a West End actor – indeed, the freedom of an unemployed West End actor – for the cabin'd, cribb'd, confin'd existence of a mere ship's steward?'

I snatched the gin from Basil's elbow and poured myself a glass.

'It was a woman, dear chappie,' he explained simply. 'I don't expect you'll remember, after that lovely medical exam you gave me before Christmas, I introduced you to my fiancée? A charming girl called Ophelia. Well, she is at the moment on board this very ship. What on earth's that rattling noise?'

'Just – just the glass against my teeth. Bit nervy these days, you know.'

'I say, you *are* in a state.' Basil took the bottle and helped himself to another drink. 'Furthermore, Ophelia hasn't the first idea in her sweet little head that I share with her this fatal and perfidious bark. Remarkable you may think?'

'Yes, very.'

'But the dear girl has such a gentle nature she would have stayed at home rather than let me sweat it out in the beastly bowels. Remind me to tell you some time, by the way, of an establishment down below known as the Glory Hole.'

I said nothing. I just stood feeling furious with the chap, popping up unexpectedly all over the place, like his blasted Demon King.

'In fact, Ophelia and I are *both* working our passage. She's doing a modelling job for the shipping adverts.' Basil arranged the cushions more comfortably under his head. 'Meanwhile, this steward lark isn't too galling, apart from the hours they make you get up in the morning. One is fed and paid, which is quite a consideration. Naturally, there are snags – someone in the Glory Hole has an electric guitar, and there's Shuttleworth, the Chief Steward. Do you know him? He'd have made an excellent assistant beak at Dotheboys' Hall.'

I nodded. I had already lavished my professional attention on Mr Shuttleworth's feet, and found him a jovial little bird emitting a friendly aura of beer and onions. I supposed it showed how people can vary with your viewpoint.

'The little wart made me scrub acres of dirty deck this morning, simply because I'd asked for Ophelia's cabin number.' Basil gave a laugh. 'Odd how our social positions have changed, Grim. I was just going to suggest that you and I and Ophelia all whooped up a few cocktails in the Veranda Bar to celebrate the reunion. Though I must say, dear chappie,' he went on warmly, 'I'm delighted Shuttleworth appointed me as your personal steward. Now I'll be able to use your cabin whenever I want, and you can't imagine how convenient it is knowing you're certain of finding a drink and a smoke. It'll be particularly useful in the afternoons, when I like to run through a few parts.'

I reached for the gin bottle again.

'A little later on –' Basil gave a wink. 'I'm sure you won't mind taking a stroll on deck while I entertain Ophelia? That sort of thing would be completely impossible in the Glory Hole, of course. Good Lord, is that the time?' He swung his legs to the deck. 'I must toil up to the bridge with the Radio Officer's sandwiches. That exploiter of the workers, Shuttleworth, lands me with all the dirty jobs. But believe me, I could put up with twice as much to be near my little Ophelia. By the way, Grim,' he added, 'whatever happened about the test?'

'Test? What test?'

'You know, when you made me widdle in a jam-jar.'

'Oh, that? Normal. Perfectly normal.'

'That's a relief. For some reason Ophelia never let me know. Terribly decent of you to invite me to make free with your cabin.' Basil put an arm round my shoulders. 'But as I always said in those happy days in the dear old digs – Grimsdyke, above all, is a gentleman.'

He left. For a minute I stood staring at the sofa. Then I pulled open the door and made straight for Mr Shuttleworth's office on the main square.

''Ullo, Doc.' The Chief Steward looked surprised over his pile of ship's papers. 'Something up? You seem proper flustered, and no mistake.'

'Something rather troublesome *has* happened, Chief,' I muttered. 'That steward you've given me –'

'Beauchamp? New this voyage. What's the perisher up to?'

'If you don't mind I'd rather not go into details. Least said, and all that. But – well, the chap isn't at all satisfactory.'

'Cor luv us, I might have known.' Mr Shuttleworth tipped back his chair. 'You wouldn't believe it, the rubbish they sends us from the Labour Exchange these days. But don't you worry, Doc. I'll shift him to the Library.'

'I don't think he should be allowed in contact with the passengers at all,' I added quickly. 'A bit familiar in his manner, you understand.'

'And so I noticed. I know his type, believe me. Right, we'll soon settle Mr Bleeding Beauchamp's hash. I'll put him waiter in the firemen's mess.'

'I'm sure that will be very much better for everybody,' I said, with a gasp of relief.

'Don't bother yourself, Doc, you won't have to look at his ugly mug again till we gets home to London. I only wish I could say the same.'

'I think that's an excellent idea, Chief. And how are the feet?'

'Much easier, thank you. Very interesting to the medical profession, I believe, my feet?'

'Absolutely fascinating.'

He chuckled. 'Fair baffled Dr O'Rory, I did, every time I took my boots off.'

'Whenever you feel you want a chat about them,' I assured him, 'just bring them along to my cabin.'

'Thank you, Doc, and so I will.' He picked up a scrap of paper. 'By the way, the Captain sent a note for you to go to the bridge when you'd finished your surgery. Nothing urgent, but he thinks he's developing a nasty cold.'

'I'll slip up at once. Thank you, Chief, for being so co-operative.'

I suddenly realized how jolly useful it had been to cast the Chief Steward's feet like bread upon the waters. Though I'd been a ghastly cad, of course, banishing old Basil somewhere among the boilers with all the firemen chucking their dinner at him. In fact, my behaviour would have made any self-respecting snake in the grass crawl rapidly away in the opposite direction. But apart from anything else, I'd have had a pretty miserable trip sharing my cabin with Richard the Third all the way to Rio de Janeiro and back. Thinking over the rush of events in the past few hours, I gave myself a little pat on the back. I had at least fixed a nice unruffled holiday, buying Ophelia long drinks in the sunshine and having a really serious bash at the tropical moonlight, and that wasn't to mention the bingo.

I climbed all those stairs feeling that I'd now an excellent chance to get myself well in with Captain Makepeace, and one never knew when such things were useful. The bridge itself seemed full of chaps in mufflers staring in all directions and drinking mugs of cocoa, and turning to a sailor polishing the fire-alarm I asked for the Captain.

A figure by the wheel lowered his binoculars.

'Doctor! You've been a devil of a long time.'

I stared at him.

'But you're not the Captain!'

'I am not the ruddy galley boy, if that's what you're inferring. And don't lean on that telegraph, unless you want to put the starboard engine full astern.'

'I – I'm frightfully sorry, sir.'

'And furthermore, Doctor, when appearing before the Captain you invariably wear your cap. Kindly remember that.'

'Yes, of course, sir.'

'*And* you offer him the courtesy of a salute. Hell's teeth!' exclaimed Captain Spratt. 'I fancy I shall have a good deal to teach you during the voyage, Doctor.'

10

I hadn't much time to consider this situation in the next few days, because everyone on board was seasick, including myself. But between holding either other people's heads or my own over vomit bowls, I kicked myself pretty hard for not examining Captain Makepeace's kidneys there and then on his desk in the shipping office.

'Captain Makepeace suffered an acute stone in the kidney on his way to the docks this morning,' Captain Spratt had informed me up on the bridge that evening. 'Most unfortunate. As our relief captains are all miles away, I like a fool volunteered.'

'It should make a pleasant break from the office, sir,' was all I could think of saying.

'My dear good feller! Like all professional mariners, I positively detest the sea.'

He took out his little silver box.

'I – er, wouldn't recommend snuff with your complaint, sir.'

'Doctor, I asked you up here to cure my cold, not to change the habits of a lifetime.'

'Yes, quite, sir.'

Fate, of course, was at it again. When I'd qualified at St Swithin's I'd uttered a great sigh of relief at finally getting out of the clutches of Sir Lancelot Spratt. Now I wasn't only back in them again, but being clutched by the whole ruddy Spratt family. Fortunately, just then somebody came up to the bridge and announced he wanted to drop the pilot, so I was able to escape and send up a couple of aspirins.

It wasn't till our fourth day out that the ship stopped throwing herself all over the ocean, and the sun returned to the sky and the colour to the passengers' cheeks. For the first time I began to think about my next meal instead of my last one, and after my morning surgery I stepped jauntily enough on deck in search of Ophelia.

I found her being photographed looking enraptured on a capstan, and what with her little blonde curls and her little brief swimsuit, I felt at once that come Captain Spratt, come seasickness, come even old Basil, it was all jolly well worth it.

'Darling, where on earth have you been to?' she greeted me.

'I've been seasick. Haven't you?'

'But of course not! I've never been sick in my life, not even after parties. Do you know Humphrey?'

She indicated a weedy chap in pink slacks with a camera, who kept saying, 'Just one more, dear, and then we'll try it on the anchor.'

'Enjoying the trip?' I asked her.

She pouted. 'A pretty dreary bunch of people, I must say.'

'I think they're supposed to get better as we go along.' I hesitated. 'You haven't seen anyone on board you know, of course?' I mentioned casually.

'But who on earth would I know on a jaunt like this?'

'No one at all, naturally,' I agreed quickly. 'And - er, I don't suppose you'll be wanting to make a tour of the ship or anything? Engine room, boilers, firemen's quarters, and so on?'

'My cabin's quite awful enough, darling, thank you.'

I nodded. 'Yes, I shouldn't penetrate the depths. Very insanitary down there. Easily catch things.'

'Another with legs, dear,' chipped in Humphrey.

'How about a cocktail in my cabin before lunch?' I suggested.

'Darling, I'd love to, but I've got to have my hair done.'

'Well, before dinner?'

'I've a date to try on some costumes for Humphrey.'

'Before lunch tomorrow, then?'

'Oh, all right, darling.'

I gave a laugh. 'After all, we've got three whole weeks ahead of us, haven't we?'

'Yes, I suppose we have, darling.'

I went back to my cabin feeling pretty pleased with myself.

But I didn't get my drink after all. After breakfast the next morning Mr Shuttleworth appeared, and announced that the Captain desired my company at twelve-thirty prompt in his cabin. I cursed a bit, but as there seemed as much chance of avoiding the summons as of avoiding the summons to the life hereafter, I scribbled a note to Ophelia putting everything off until dinner time and dutifully climbed to the bridge.

'Ah, Doctor! There you are.'

I entered the Captain's cabin, saluting hard enough to dislocate my right wrist joint.

'I thought I'd have you up here for a drink,' he explained.

'That's very civil of you, sir,' I returned, as politely as possible.

'Get to know you a bit, you understand?'

He paused to give his nose a couple of helpings of snuff.

'That cold of mine, Doctor. Gone like a flash.'

'I'm delighted to hear it, sir.'

'Good job of work. I regard it as one of the first principles in successfully commanding a vessel at sea always to give credit where credit is due. I do so now.'

At least the old boy seemed much more affable. Now he was like Blackbeard after a good lunch settling down to organize the walking the plank.

'You were a student of my brother's, eh?' the Captain went on, as I took a seat. 'The brains of the family. The bookworm, at any rate. I suppose I really should look him up in London. I've no excuse, having time enough on my hands now I've swallowed the anchor.'

He whisked up more snuff, making rather a noise about it.

'As for you, Doctor, you know the rules. Observe them, and you and I will get on perfectly well on board.'

'I'm sure we shall, sir,' I told him hopefully.

'You're not interested in the Great Pyramid, I suppose?'

'Not in the slightest, sir.'

'Good.'

I began to feel the outlook was fairly encouraging. I

should have to be pretty discreet with Ophelia, of course, but a ship is crammed with cosy nooks for little chats. And though old Basil wasn't far away, being chased round the boilers every time the menu didn't come up to scratch, as far as Ophelia was concerned they might have been in two different ships sailing in opposite directions.

'Now let's have our drink.' The Captain interrupted my thoughts by clapping his hands and calling, 'Steward!'

And there was that blasted chap Basil again, standing in the doorway.

'Anything the matter, Doctor?' exclaimed the Captain.

'Nothing – nothing, sir. Just a little rigor. Possibly a slight temperature.'

'You must look after yourself. We can't have the doctor sick, you know.'

'No, of course not, sir.'

I stared hard at Basil. He stared hard at the silver chronometer over my head. I wondered for a few seconds if it really was the beastly fellow, or whether I'd got hallucinations from general break-up of the psychology under the strain. He seemed different from the chap who'd been sprawling on my sofa guzzling my gin – older, somehow, more bent, and half asleep.

'Name your tipple Doctor,' invited Captain Spratt genially, blowing his nose on a large red-spotted handkerchief.

'Pink gin,' I muttered.

'And for me, as usual, Beauchamp.'

'I have taken the liberty of anticipating your wishes, sir,' replied Basil, advancing with a tray and two glasses.

'But, damn it! What about the doctor's wishes –'

'I took the further liberty of anticipating those, sir.'

'The man's a marvel,' muttered Captain Spratt.

'I trust that is the quantity of angostura bitters you favour, sir?' went on Basil, bending over me with the glass.

I glared at him.

'Will there be anything more, sir?' he asked the Captain.

'Not for the moment, thank you, Beauchamp.'

'Thank *you*, sir.'

He withdrew, with the dignity of a High Court judge knocking off for lunch.

'Don't see many fellers at sea like him, eh?' Captain Spratt gave an appreciative nod. 'In the old days, you could have swapped the Captain's tiger for the butler in any stately home in the kingdom, and no one would have been the wiser. Now they're all scent and hair oil and what's-me-overtime. But Beauchamp's one of the real old type. I don't suppose you even see 'em ashore now, more's the pity.'

'I don't seem to have noticed him about the ship much,' was all I managed to say, struggling to adjust myself to the situation.

'Of course you haven't. Do you know where that fool of a Chief Steward buried him? Down below in the firemen's mess, if you please. I spotted the feller on my rounds yesterday, and brought him on deck.'

There was a cough from the doorway.

'Yes, Beauchamp?'

'I have removed the cover of your bunk, sir, and set out your bedroom slippers, should you feel the inclination for a rest after luncheon, sir.'

The Captain nodded. 'It's very likely I'll turn in.'

'If I might respectfully point out, sir, a short sleep in the afternoon has been advocated by many distinguished men of affairs. I would mention Napoleon and Mr Gladstone, sir.'

'I can perfectly well understand it, Beauchamp.'

'I shall call you at four o'clock precisely, sir.'

'Very good, Beauchamp.'

'With a pot of tea and assorted confectionery, sir.'

'Thank you, Beauchamp.'

'Thank *you*, sir.'

Basil disappeared again.

The whole scene left me totally mystified. Particularly as Basil was such a lazy hound in the digs he'd hardly ever make his own bed, and certainly never anyone else's.

'Beauchamp will be an absolute godsend at the party tonight,' I heard the Captain saying.

'Party?' I looked up. 'What party?'

'The usual jamboree – Captain's cocktails. Bores me to tears myself, but the passengers expect it. Just a few from the first-class, you understand. I've asked the crowd from my table and that advertising woman and the feller with the pink pants.'

I gave a jump. 'Not up *here*, sir?'

Captain Spratt glared at me. 'I am not in the habit of entertaining my guests on the bridge or the fo'c'sle head, if that's what you infer.'

'No, no, of course not, sir, but –'

'You are naturally invited, so kindly be sure you've got a clean dickey. Six o'clock sharp, if you please.'

'I – I don't think I'll be able to attend, sir.'

'You don't think you'll what?' roared the Captain.

'I mean, I've a good bit of work to clear up down below, sir –'

'Now look here, Doctor. If you think I am going to make footling small talk over the olives to a bunch of third-class people with first-class tickets, without the full and enthusiastic support of every one of my senior officers, you are greatly mistaken. Hell's teeth! I will not have any shillyshallying. I will not have it! You will arrange your work efficiently, and be here on time. That is an order.'

'Of course, sir. Quite, sir. I assure you it will be a great pleasure, sir –'

'It certainly will not be. But if you don't make it appear so to everybody present, God help you.' He swallowed the rest of his gin. 'Now I must go to the bridge.'

The Captain disappeared up a ladder. I hung behind for a second or two. Then I nipped back to the little pantry outside his cabin door, to find Basil enjoying a smoke and helping himself to the gin.

'Look here! What's the ruddy idea?' I demanded at once.

'My dear chappie!' He gave a grin. 'How was I?'

'What the hell do you mean, how were you?' I felt pretty narked at it all. 'You not only give me the fright of my life creeping through the doorway, but you go oiling round the Captain like a stage butler –'

'But that's exactly it! Don't you remember the very first show I was in? *The Missing Butler*. I played the butler. In fact, now I come to think of it, I've been playing butlers steadily ever since, when I've been in work. I've become absolutely first-class at this "Dinner is served, m'lord, Coffee is on the terrace, m'lady, The body awaits you in the library, Inspector" stuff. Though you can't imagine how hard it is living, breathing and thinking a butler from morning to night. I'm so glad you liked the performance.'

'The way you were carrying on certainly made the Admirable Crichton look like a teashop waitress,' I told him, 'but that's not the point –'

'Thank you, dear chappie. You know how I appreciate a good notice. The idea came to me when I was relegated to the firemen's mess by slave driver Shuttleworth. Not that it was too bad down there, once I'd stopped being beastly sick. All the firemen these days are little skinny men, you know, with clean collars who turn knobs. But as I wasn't allowed on the passenger decks, the whole object of my voyage was defeated. After all,' he explained, 'the only reason I'm floating about the place like this is to be near my Ophelia.'

I said nothing.

'And tonight,' laughed Basil, 'the poor dear thing is going to get the surprise of her sweet young life. I can hardly imagine her face when she steps through that door and sees me waiting with her first Martini. No end of a joke, don't you think? Though not a word if you happen to see her about the ship,' he added darkly. 'Sorry I can't offer you another gin. I must go down to the Glory Hole for a bite of lunch myself.'

'If you think you can go on pulling wool over the eyes of a chap like Captain Spratt –'

'What do you make of our bearded chum in the gold braid, by the way? Rather preposterous, isn't he? Still, the experience is no end of help. I might easily find myself playing a captain sometime, and I'm picking up all sorts of useful hints just watching him prowling about.'

II

I went down to the first-class saloon. I was almost too worried to eat, and I'd all that seasickness to catch up with, too. Mumbling a few polite words, I sat down and unfolded my table-napkin and fiddled a bit with the menu.

I had my own table not far from Ophelia and Humphrey, with three eating companions. On my right, Miss Miggs, a schoolteacher recovering from her thyroid being removed. On my left, Mr Bridgenorth, who seemed to be some sort of high-powered grocer. Opposite, Mrs van Barn, a pleasant American who looked as though she'd been turned out by a posh beauty parlour, though without making them work too hard for their money.

At least I hadn't the extra strain of making conversation, because everyone meeting a doctor socially is bursting to pour out their entire clinical history since the mumps. Miss Miggs kicked off with the story of her thyroidectomy, which they'd issued invitations for surgeons all over London to see, like a film premiere. She was followed by Mr Bridgenorth, who'd been packed off on a cruise when the strain of flogging all those packets of cornflakes got too much for his blood pressure. And though Mrs van Barn was healthy enough herself she'd lost a couple of husbands through highly complicated diseases, and it struck me they must have been pretty rich chaps at that, affording to have them at New York rates.

While the three of them swapped symptoms over the roast pork, I simply threw in the sympathetic word and wondered what the devil to do about the coming evening. Somehow I had to keep Basil and Ophelia asunder. As I couldn't very well stop Basil's appearance at the party, short of telling the Captain he was suffering from some frightful contagious disease, it was clear I had to go to work pretty smartly on Ophelia.

Immediately after lunch I searched the ship, and discovered her looking enraptured against the funnel.

'What ho, there!'

I waited till Humphrey was busy fiddling with his camera.

'Haven't forgotten the little drink rearranged for this evening, I hope?' I asked.

'Oh, darling, it's a frightful bore, but I can't possibly make it. I've just had a simply lovely invitation to the Captain's cocktail party, all covered with flags and things.'

'Not the Captain's cocktail party!'

I put on a look of horror I doubt even Basil could have bettered.

'But you're not really going?' I demanded.

'Why ever not?' They say it's the absolute social pinnacle of the voyage. Ascot and Cowes all rolled into one.'

'Oh, Lord, no! It's a frightfully dreary affair. Everyone knows that the people at the Captain's table are always the stuffiest bunch on board. They just stand round talking about stocks and shares and golf and downing all the free gin. You might just as well be at a cocktail party in Bagshot.'

'I happen to have been to some wonderful parties in Bagshot, darling. When I was engaged to a divine officer at Sandhurst.'

This was a new one on me, but I went on, 'You'll be absolutely bored to tears –'

'It happens I particularly want to go,' said Ophelia firmly. 'I can always have a drink with you another day, can't I? After all,' she added, after a pause, 'neither of us is likely to go away for the week-end or anything.'

'No, of course not. But Ophelia –'

'A little more of the bosom, please dear,' said Humphrey, restarting operations.

'Ophelia –'

'Sorry, darling. I'm busy.'

I went back to my cabin. I knew that once Ophelia made up her mind about anything she was as difficult to shift as

Captain Spratt himself. I paced up and down and finished my tin of duty-free cigarettes. I stared through the port-hole, wondering if some typhoon might blow up and cancel the whole affair. I cursed the ruddy ship and the whole ruddy sea. I'd started the voyage as blithe as a newly-hatched seagull, and now I'd the stickiest situation imaginable on my hands. I supposed it was just the same with the Ancient Mariner.

The afternoon passed. I tried to distract myself by having a go at Sir Lancelot's memoirs. I took evening surgery as usual in the ship's hospital. At last it was time to put on my little mess jacket and stiff shirt, and as I did up my tie I decided that only desperate measures were left.

Going aloft towards the Captain's cabin I slipped into a little nook I remembered below his companion-way, between the officers' oilskin locker and the gyrocompass. As the guests started to arrive I kept peering round the corner for Ophelia, until I began to wonder if I'd had a stroke of luck and she had gone to bed with a nasty headache. But, of course, she was always late for everything, and I could hear everyone chatting away brightly up in the cabin by the time I spotted her coming down the deck.

'Darling!' She gave a shriek as I jumped out of the shadows. 'What on earth's the matter with you these days? You're always going about frightening the life out of me. Is it your idea of shock treatment, or something?'

'A word with you,' I announced solemnly. 'Alone.'

She looked alarmed. 'But why in heaven's name all the mystery? Is the ship sinking, or something?'

'It's a bit difficult to explain out here,' I mumbled. 'If you'd care to nip down to my cabin for that drink –'

'Well, I like that!' Ophelia stamped her foot. 'I happen to have been especially looking forward to this party, *and* I've put on a new dress. How you have the damned nerve to suggest I utterly waste my evening –'

'I thought it would be rather nice for us to have a chat,' I persisted, edging nearer. 'After all, Ophelia old girl, we haven't seen much of each other on board, have we? And what with my taking all that trouble to be on the ship with you –'

'You make me sick! For once in my life I've a chance to get away from it all and meet some nice interesting new people, and you have to come panting after me like an over-sexed bloodhound –'

'Ophelia!' This was all jolly galling. 'Ophelia, surely you understand my feelings towards you –'

'I understand them only too well.'

'Dash it! I told you once how I absolutely wanted to marry you –'

'And I can tell you now there's not the slightest possibility of my ever being idiotic enough to allow you to ruin my entire life. All I ask is for you to stop ruining my entire holiday. I'm going up to that party.'

I grabbed her arm.

'Take your hands off me this instant, you beast! Or I'll scream for a sailor.'

'Ophelia –' I hissed. 'Let me tell you exactly why you're not to go up there tonight.'

'Please do. No one would be more delighted to find out than myself.'

'Basil – Basil Beauchamp – is in the Captain's cabin.'

She stared at me.

'Yes. I saw him there. With my own eyes, this very morning.'

'But – but what on earth is *he* doing on board? And hobnobbing with the Captain, too?'

'He isn't hobnobbing. He's serving the drinks.'

'Serving the drinks?'

I explained briefly the terms of Basil's steamship ticket.

'Of all the stupid idiotic oafs!' Ophelia stamped the deck again. 'Why the hell can't he leave me alone? Why the hell can't you both leave me alone? Aren't I allowed to have a scrap of private life and talk sometimes to other men than you pair of –'

'At least you can't possibly show your face at the party,' I interrupted.

'And why shouldn't I show my face wherever I damn well like?'

'I mean, Basil in his little white jacket –'

'If Basil wants to turn himself into a floating waiter,

that's his concern. I am going up to that party, and you, my fine friend, will escort me. Come on!'

'Now – now just a minute, Ophelia.' I started to back away. 'I mean, if you don't think me rather rude, it would be better all round if I simply went down to my cabin –'

'Come on – worm!'

She grabbed my arm. We went up the companion-way, her nails biting into my left biceps.

I don't know whether Basil expected Ophelia to throw her arms round his neck, burst into tears diluting his tray of Martinis, or to faint. As it happened, she simply swept up, said, 'Martini, steward,' and swept off again.

I edged into the background, watching Basil trying to make all this out. Never a quick thinker off the boards, he frowned a bit and seemed to decide that Ophelia simply hadn't noticed his face. I suppose that was reasonable enough. You don't usually go to parties peering round the waiters in case one of them happens to be your fiancé. Ophelia meanwhile struck up conversation with Captain Spratt, though talking and laughing rather louder than usual, and what with it being a low cabin and it being Ophelia, this was pretty noisy altogether.

'Captain, what an absolutely divine party, and how terribly sweet of you to ask me,' she prattled.

'But I am sure, Miss O'Brien, you must find it an extremely dull affair.'

The Captain was clearly tickled to the ends of his whiskers at Ophelia making a dart for him, particularly in that low-cut dress.

'I have no doubt that in London you are greatly in demand to grace far more brilliant assemblies than I can provide,' he went on.

'But Captain, I lead the quietest of lives.' She gazed up at him. 'I'm quite a home-body, you know. Just cooking and knitting and the television. That's why it's so wonderful to be on board your lovely exciting ship.'

Basil came squarely up to her, pushing his way through the other guests and staring hard under his eyebrows, like Boris Karloff in the old film posters.

'Steward,' said Ophelia, snapping her fingers. 'Nuts.'

Basil stood still, breathing heavily.

'Beauchamp, there are guests with empty glasses in the corner,' ordered the Captain. 'Attend to them, if you please.'

'And just to think, Captain, you're in charge of all this great big liner,' Ophelia continued. 'Doesn't the strain keep you awake all night?'

Captain Spratt smiled. 'I am glad to tell you, dear lady, that since first assuming command I have never suffered a moment of insomnia. Though, naturally, the position has its responsibilities –'

'But Captain, you're just the type who simply thrives on responsibilities.' She gave a big sigh. 'You'd be absolutely surprised at the spineless creatures I have to mix with in London. Some I could mention would make a jellyfish look like the sentries outside Buckingham Palace. But you, Captain –' She patted his lapel. 'You're a man of action, anyone could see that.'

The Captain took a pinch of snuff.

'Beauchamp – those glasses,' he repeated.

'What broad shoulders you have, Captain,' breathed Ophelia.

'Madam.' Basil poked a dish towards her. 'Your nuts.'

'Thank you, steward.'

'Madam –'

'Yes, steward?'

'Is – is that all, madam?'

'Definitely all, steward. Don't you think it atrocious,' Ophelia went on to Captain Spratt, 'how these days some men will pursue a woman right to the very ends of the earth?'

'I'm afraid I'm hardly qualified to answer that, Miss O'Brien, being a confirmed bachelor. Indeed, I have never never pursued a woman in my life, except for an unfortunate lady who became unhinged at Teneriffe some years ago and raced round the deck in her shift.'

'With great respect, madam,' intruded Basil, 'I would venture the opinion that some ladies ought to regard it as a compliment to be followed anywhere at all.'

Ophelia raised her eyebrows. 'Indeed?'

'And that's assuming the lady in question were worthy of the gentleman's attentions, madam.'

The Captain gave a short laugh. 'A very philosophical character, our Beauchamp. Quite like that famous feller in the books – what's his name? – Jeeves.'

'Are you suggesting,' continued Ophelia, fixing Basil with her eye like a winkle on the end of a pin, 'that a lady might not be good enough for some mean-minded moron who won't let her out of his sight for more than five minutes?'

'I would only say –'

'Thank you, Beauchamp,' said Captain Spratt briefly. 'That will be all.'

'I would only say,' Basil went on doggedly, 'that the gentleman would be surprised and pained at the lady not wanting him to accompany her – at considerable trouble and discomfort to himself –'

'The gentleman's an idiot,' snapped Ophelia.

'Unless, of course, the lady had the firm intention, once out of his sight, of cutting fast and loose –'

'What a beastly suggestion!'

'That will do, Beauchamp!' roared Captain Spratt.

I suddenly realized everyone else in the cabin had stopped talking. I edged even deeper into the background and grabbed another Martini.

'Furthermore, madam,' Basil went on, now getting warmed up, 'if a gentleman wishes to keep his self-respect –'

'Self-respect? Ha! Don't make me laugh. How you can imagine anyone would have a scrap of self-respect after rolling about in pink tights and a red nose in disgusting pantomimes –'

'It was *not* a disgusting pantomime! It was an extremely high-class show. It simply didn't happen to be appreciated in the district –'

'It was a fifth-rate road show which anyone with the slightest pretensions of being an actor –'

'I – the gentleman – *is* an actor, damn it! You just wait, madam!' Basil shook his finger, spilling all the nuts. 'You just wait. One day you'll see him with top billing in the West End and you'll be so blasted sorry –'

'Steward!' Captain Spratt made all the Martini glasses rattle. 'Go below at once!'

'I'm sorry,' muttered Basil, 'extremely sorry. I apologize to everyone. It's simply that I have an urgent message from this lady's fiancé –'

'Go below, I say! Miss O'Brien, I really must express my regrets for this most painful interruption. If you have had a message by wireless –'

'It didn't come by wireless,' Basil interrupted, 'it came by telepathy.'

'Good God, he's mad,' muttered the Captain. 'Where's the doctor?'

'Mad as a hatter,' agreed Ophelia briskly, 'because I have no fiancé. Now, Captain, what were we discussing before we were so rudely interrupted?'

'Ophelia – !'

Basil sank on one knee, like an obedient camel.

'Doctor! Get this man out of here. Hell's teeth! He's raving. Absolutely raving. I'm extremely sorry, ladies and gentlemen, extremely sorry. This is a most unhappy interruption to your evening –'

'Ophelia – !'

'I say, Basil old lad,' I hissed in his ear. 'There doesn't seem much doubt this is the cue for your exit.'

'I refuse to leave this cabin until I have had a proper explanation and apology,' Basil went on, staring round wildly.

'Right,' said the Captain. 'Mr Shuttleworth! Send for the Bos'n.'

'Look here –' began Basil.

But even then we had to call the Quartermaster and a couple of sailors to get the poor chap decently out of sight.

I must say, it struck me the idiot had made a first-class mess of his evening. Apart from anything else, it rather looked as though he'd gone and talked himself out of a nice cushy job to back among those boilers.

12

'That's one scene I'd never play again,' said Basil bitterly. 'Not for top billing in London and Broadway, I wouldn't.'

'A bit harrowing for you, I must say,' I agreed, 'not to mention the audience.'

It was about an hour later. I'd taken him straight down to the ship's hospital, where I was still treating him with large gins.

'But I can't understand it! The last time I saw Ophelia she was so terribly sweet and loving.'

'Possibly it was the shock of running into you like that. Unbalances the psychology sometimes.'

'You're absolutely sure you didn't tip her off, or anything?' demanded Basil.

I shook my head. 'Not a word. Hardly know her, really. Just see her about the ship.'

He fell silent for a moment.

'Quite a coincidence that you should be on board, too, Grim?'

I shifted slightly. 'Tricks of fate, you know, tricks of fate.'

'I mean, in London neither you nor I nor Ophelia knew we were all going to be in the same boat, if you follow me.'

'It's always pleasant to meet old friends unexpectedly anywhere.'

There was another pause.

'It all confirms my darkest suspicions,' said Basil.

'Suspicions?'

He glared into his glass, looking like Othello coming to the smothering bit.

'I fear, Grim, there is . . . well, what's generally referred to in domestic drama as "someone else".'

'Oh, ah?'

'Dear chappie!' Basil burst out. 'Do you know why I *really* came on this trip?'

'To be near Ophelia –'

'But that's only half of it.'

He felt inside his white jacket, and produced the shipping brochure Ophelia had brought to the consulting room.

'Look at this. The day Ophelia wrote about her new job, I spotted the thing in a travel agent's up at Blackport. I expect you've read it?'

I nodded.

'I'm not what you'd call an abnormally jealous type,' Basil went on.

'I certainly hope – I'm certain you're not.'

'Now I come to think of it, nobody is on the stage. Except about themselves, of course. And it's not that I don't trust Ophelia.'

'No, of course not.'

'But . . . well, she's a highly attractive girl.'

'Very,' I agreed.

'Of a warm and affectionate nature.'

'I'll say she – is she, indeed?'

'Not to mention being highly susceptible to romantic surroundings.'

'Odd, I'd never thought of that one.'

'But if she started dancing round the deck in the tropical moonlight with chappies in white dinner jackets – there's a picture of them here – there's no knowing what I'd . . . I mean, if anyone so much as laid a finger on her . . .'

It suddenly occurred to me what a big chap Basil was. Now I came to think of it, whenever he was behind with the rent in the digs he was always currying favour by hauling up the coals or shifting the landlady's grand piano.

'I suppose I should really be thoroughly civilized and understanding about it all,' he added.

'Often the best way in the end.'

'I should simply retire with sadness and dignity.'

'I think that would be terribly impressive.'

'But I couldn't. Not with anyone meddling with my little Ophelia. Instead, I'd break his rotten neck.'

I reached for the gin bottle.

'Though Lord knows if I'll ever see her again on board.' Basil sadly replaced the folder. 'That tyrant Shuttleworth will have something a damn sight worse up his sleeve than the firemen's mess. It was a pretty good job up top, too, once I'd discovered the old boy wanted a glass of sea-water for his teeth at night, and so on.'

'Look here, old lad –'

I couldn't help feeling sorry for the poor fellow. I also couldn't help feeling it might be a good thing to build up a little friendliness.

'You just leave it all to me, Basil,' I told him. 'I'll nip up to the Captain and simply say you were overcome with a sort of nervous breakdown, entirely due to overwork in his service. In a way it's perfectly true, and I can blind him with a bit of science. Then perhaps they'll fix you up with some quiet easy job somewhere on the strength of it.'

'Dear chappie!' He seized my hand. 'Do you think it would work?'

'Absolutely certain of it. After all, I'm the doctor.'

'I'd be eternally grateful.'

'No trouble at all, I assure you.'

'Good old Grim!' Actors are emotional birds, and for a moment I was scared he was going to have a jolly good blub. 'Even those days in the dear old digs, I always knew one thing – I could count on you, at least, as a real true chum.'

'Oh, tut,' I said lightly.

All this really made me feel a stinking cad, of course. But I suppose taking to deceit is like taking to drink – after a time you get so full of it, you hardly notice a bit more. So I packed Basil off to the Glory Hole, adjusted my tie, and climbed again up all those stairs to the Captain's cabin, preparing some sort of tale to pitch on his behalf.

I reckoned the party should have been over by then, and was rather surprised as I tapped on the door to hear a burst of female laughter inside.

'Enter!'

There was the old boy tucking into roast chicken and asparagus, with a bottle of champagne at his elbow and

Mr Shuttleworth himself in attendance. Sharing the binge with him was Ophelia.

'Ah, Doctor! What have you done with that dangerous lunatic? Securely under lock and key, I hope? I should have known the feller was unbalanced. I remember now the peculiar way he kept snooping at me round corners.'

'I hope I'm not interrupting anything sir?' I remarked, shooting Ophelia a bit of a glance.

'Not at all, Doctor, not at all. It is simply that I felt my appearance in the saloon might prove somewhat embarrassing after tonight's events, and I decided to dine up here. This charming young lady kindly consented to share my simple meal.'

'The Captain has been telling me the most absolutely thrilling things about the ship,' said Ophelia. 'Haven't you, Captain?'

The Captain suddenly seemed to become all gold braid and medals.

'It is the Master's duty to answer his passengers' questions, my dear Miss O'Brien. But perhaps for the first time in my life at sea I can say it is a positive pleasure as well.' He raised his champagne glass. 'By the way, Doctor, if you want to put that feller Beauchamp in a straitjacket, it is perfectly all right with me.'

I gave a little cough. 'I agree, sir, the unfortunate man is slightly off balance mentally –'

'You can say that again,' murmured Ophelia.

'But I assure you it's only a temporary condition. It was the strain, sir, being over-conscientious about his work.'

Captain Spratt grunted.

'If I might suggest, sir, he should continue with some simple job down below suitable for his limited mental capacities.'

He stroked his beard.

'Oh, the poor thing's perfectly harmless,' said Ophelia suddenly. I didn't know if she was beginning to feel sorry over the way she'd treated Basil, or merely beginning to feel drunk. 'Give him some nice easy work, Captain, where he can fuddle along in his own little way.'

'H'm.'

There was a pause.

'Oh, very well, very well. Mr Shuttleworth!'

'Sir?'

'You heard that conversation. Put Beauchamp somewhere where he can't come to any harm. Just see he won't get under *my* feet, that's all I ask. Thank you, Doctor. Good night.'

'Bye bye, Doctor dear,' said Ophelia.

As I left, I fancied they were just about to pull the wishbone.

13

The situation on board now struck me as reasonably under control. I felt that Basil had copped it so hard from Ophelia he'd left me free to oil my way back into her affections. And though the poor fellow had made a first-class idiot of himself, he'd probably done no worse out of his eruption than taking charge of the stewards' wash-house. It seemed very satisfactory all round.

I was therefore rather shaken at lunch the following day to find the chap handing me my soup.

'How the devil did you get here?' I demanded.

'The Chief Steward's express orders, sir,' replied Basil, wiping his thumb.

'Chief Steward's orders? But shouldn't you be somewhere down among the entrails?'

'The Chief Steward considered this post would be the most convenient not only for me, sir, but for everyone else.'

It was all that fool Shuttleworth's fault. Working everything out carefully, he'd made Basil a saloon waiter on my table, so I'd be nice and handy in case he ran riot again.

'Fish and chips,' I told him, pretty tersely.

There seemed nothing to do but shoulder the situation.

I suppose Basil had been living, breathing and thinking a waiter all morning, but either his heart wasn't in the part or through emotional strain he was losing his touch, because he gave a ruddy awful performance. He was passable on the 'I-hear-personally-from-the-Chef-the-roast-beef-is-excellent-today' business, but he got into frightful trouble trying to serve the boiled potatoes one-handed and having to chase them all over the table with his fork. Then he kept forgetting which door to the pantry was In or Out, the butter got stuck on the point of his knife, he had oranges rolling all over the deck like tennis balls, and on the whole it was a pretty miserable lunch.

And not only through Mr Shuttleworth's bad casting.

A strange gloom had come over my eating mates, apart from their having run out of symptoms. In fact, a strange gloom had come over the whole ruddy ship. It was all the fault of Jeremy in the curly bowler and his devilish pals.

Anyone stumbling on a Capricorn Line poster through a London fog probably had to be physically restrained from selling up his home on the spot and buying a ticket for the next boat. And from that little brochure thing, a trip in a Capricorn ship made the seventh heaven of the Mohammedans like a walk in the park on a rainy Sunday afternoon. But when you come down to it, all passenger ships are just our dear old friend the English seaside hotel, with music in the palm court, thick and clear for dinner, and everyone's favourite chair in the lounge. Except that in a seaside hotel you can always escape for a bit, for a nice bracing stroll all alone to the local at the end of the prom. And another thing. Those curly-bowler chaps had rather naughtily tended to stress sex in their advertisements, this being what people in England are most interested in, after a spot of sunshine, of course. Everyone came on board expecting to meet men like those coves in white dinner jackets or girls like Ophelia, and when they only saw the same people on the morning train to Town in their swimming-trunks, they began to feel they'd been rather done over the price of their ticket. This fell particularly hard on Mr Bridgenorth, who in forty years hadn't found time to get married, and on Miss Miggs, who in forty years hadn't been asked, particularly as they'd just discovered they both came from opposite ends of the same street in Dulwich.

'No morning papers at sea,' grumbled Mr Bridgenorth over the fish.

'No telly,' added Miss Miggs.

'Can't even sit on the deck in peace. Nothing but screaming kids and gossiping women and rope quoits hitting you in the neck every five minutes. You might as well be at the end of Southend Pier on August Bank Holiday.'

'I can't say I go for their six-course luncheons,' sighed Mrs van Barn, who seemed to be keeping the most cheerful under the strain. 'How do you imagine they get every single thing to taste like boiled knitting? I guess this refrigerated fish has been floating a darn sight longer on top of the ocean than underneath it.'

'As for the faultless service – !' cried Mr Bridgenorth, as Basil dropped Sauce Hollandaise down his lap.

'Give the steward a break,' urged Mrs van Barn amiably. 'The poor guy's doing his best. Aren't you Steward?'

'One endeavours to give satisfaction, madam,' murmured Basil, briskly mopping Mr Bridgenorth.

'Sure you do. Here, let me help. A drop of cleaner and a sponge and these pants will look better than new in no time.'

'Thank you, madam.'

'Why, you're welcome, Steward. That's what we're here on earth for, isn't it, to help each other?'

Basil, the wicked chap, gave a bit of a flutter to his eyelashes.

'A most admirable philosophy, if I may take the liberty of saying so, madam.'

'Say, isn't he cute?' Mrs van Barn smiled round the table. 'What's your name, Steward?'

'Beauchamp, madam.'

'No, I mean your first name.'

'Basil, madam.'

'Basil? Gee, that's lovely. I can't say I've ever known a man called Basil.'

'Thank you, madam. Chips?'

I didn't think much about this little *tête-à-tête* until we all trooped in for dinner. Our Mrs van Barn always managed to measure up to those advertisements in the *New Yorker*, but that night she appeared looking absolutely smashing in her best dress and best hair. She sat down and stared at Basil like something in Cartier's window, and got him to bring her every item on the menu.

'Say, let me show you how to do it,' she volunteered, when the poor chap was struggling with those blasted potatoes again. 'See here, it's easy.'

We all admitted that Mrs van Barn was a pretty handy potato server. But after that she started helping Basil dishing out the duck, and what with her mixing the salad and sweeping up the breadcrumbs and fetching the butter from the table next door, people began to notice. Particularly Mr Shuttleworth, who went red in the face and hovered rather, but as Mrs van Barn had the most expensive suite on board he couldn't do much about it.

And Ophelia noticed, too.

14

'Gaston, darling.'

Ophelia slipped her arm through mine as we left the saloon after dinner the following evening.

'Who's that ghastly fat woman with the purple hair sitting opposite you?'

'Mrs Sybil van Barn? A decent enough soul, though rather heavy on the husbands.'

'Terribly vulgar, don't you think, the way she hobnobs with the waiters?'

'Oh, I don't know,' I replied sportingly. 'Americans are always pretty pally with their servitors, and *vice versa*. Even in the plushiest New York restaurants the chap comes up with a deep bow and asks, "*Que voulez-vous*, bud?".'

Ophelia pouted.

'I mean, if Basil really wants to go round the world being a waiter, he ought to learn to keep his position as one.'

'First of all he ought to learn to serve boiled potatoes, if you ask me.'

'Darling,' said Ophelia, 'would you like to buy me a liqueur in the Veranda Bar?'

'Who, me? I say! Would I, indeed! My dear old girl, come along.'

'How terribly sweet of you.' Ophelia put her little hand into mine. 'Darling, I'm *so* glad you're aboard.'

I'd previously decided to let things drift between us until at least the scars she'd made had healed on my left biceps. I was still in love with her, of course. You couldn't help it. After all, it had taken her only ten minutes to get someone like Captain Spratt rolling with his paws in the air at her feet. This seemed a terrific chance to reopen the attack, particularly as we'd now got into the tropical moonlight belt.

Ophelia sat with a *crème de menthe* in a *chaise longue,* chatting away as brightly as in the old days. And I must say I felt pretty pleased with myself, particularly with all those envious glances from the chaps as they passed.

'I'm sorry I was so beastly to you the other night,' she apologized. 'The stupid way Basil behaved quite made me lose my head. You know how it is.'

'Let's just forget the whole little episode, shall we?'

I patted her hand.

'After all, darling, you were terribly kind to me all those weeks I was quite alone in London.'

'And I hope,' I told her, patting a bit harder, 'I can be even kinder when we get back.'

'Darling, you're so sweet,' said Ophelia.

I felt that as far as bliss was concerned, this was just the job.

'If you're not too tired after being photographed hanging from the rails all day,' I ventured, deciding to strike while the iron was fair sizzling. 'Perhaps you'd like a go at the Gala Dance?'

'But darling, I'd adore to! I haven't danced with you all the trip, have I? It'll be quite like old times.'

I couldn't remember a more rapturous evening, particularly as I knew there wouldn't be one of those sinister chaps sidling up with the bill at the end of it. Meanwhile, the tropical moonlight at least had come out as advertised, and I could hardly wait for an appropriate moment to suggest we combed the streamers out of our hair and went for a little stroll round the deck.

'How divine!' breathed Ophelia, as we paused in a nook between the starboard fan house and a ventilator.

I swallowed a bit. What with the soft swish of the water, and the stars, and the little breeze flicking through her hair, chaps get a bit overcome.

'Care for a chat?' I murmured, edging farther into the nook.

She stroked my lapels. 'Gaston – you're such a dear.'

'Ophelia, my darling.' I tickled her left ear. 'This is the

very moment I've been living for since I came aboard.'

'You came aboard for *me*, darling,' she remembered softly.

'For you, my sweet.' I shifted the tickling to her mastoid bone. 'For you alone have I adopted the perilous existence –'

'Kiss me, darling.'

I hastened to oblige. But at that moment a voice from the other side of the ventilator said, 'Gee, Basil, you sure have made my trip.'

'And you, my dear Sybil, have certainly made my year.'

Ophelia snapped her teeth shut so fiercely she pretty well took off the end of my nose.

'Basil dear!' There was a sigh behind the ventilator. 'You're a wonderful man. It's a crying shame you having to go around just being a steward like this.'

'It's only a temporary part – I mean a temporary post. Better things are in store.'

'There sure will be, dear, if I have anything to do with it. Kiss me again.'

'Of all the dirty little worms!' hissed Ophelia. 'My own fiancé, too!'

'I'm afraid the chap's a bit of a cad,' I muttered.

'You just wait till I get my hands –'

'Here, wait a second – !'

I grabbed her dress. Knowing Ophelia, if she started a scene on deck they'd have to send for the Bos'n with his fire hoses before she finished it.

'I'm going to tear that skunk limb from –'

'But creating in public!' I whispered urgently. 'It's frightfully undignified.'

'I couldn't care less how damn undignified –'

'I mean, undignified in front of – of *her*.'

The point struck home. Ophelia stood breathing heavily. Before she could change her mind, I seized her hand and led her briskly down the deck.

'Surely, it's far better,' I murmured stroking it soothingly, as we hurried past the lifeboats. 'Simply to summon Basil to your cabin and give him it good and proper in the ear tomorrow morning?'

Ophelia bit her lip.

'I've half a mind to push him over the rail here and now, and laugh while the sharks eat him.'

'Strong feelings,' I agreed, as we stopped in the stern, 'are perfectly understandable in the circumstances.'

'With that overweight adventuress who's already murdered two husbands –'

'If I may be of any help in your distress,' I reminded her, 'you can rely on me.'

'Dear Gaston!' She threw her arms round my neck. 'You're so upright and honest.'

'Come, now –'

'Yes! So honourable in your dealings with women.'

'One has one's code, naturally.'

'It's so wonderful to have someone in the whole world to trust and to admire!'

'But it is you, Ophelia, who bring out the best in me,' I explained, very civilly. 'And now if you'd like to continue our stroll, there's always the other side of the ship.'

'I'm far too upset,' she announced. 'It's all given me a beastly headache, and I must go to bed. Good night.'

She disappeared.

I must say, I felt a bit narked with that idiot Basil, ruining my evening again. But, I told myself as I went down to my own cabin, now there was always tomorrow. If Basil didn't disappear over the side to the sharks, he'd certainly disappear just as completely from Ophelia's life. To be replaced, I reflected as I put my feet on the sofa and poured myself a gin, by that upright, honest, reliable, honourable chap, Gaston Grimsdyke.

'Poor old Basil,' I murmured. I felt quite sorry for the fellow.

I had another gin, and pictured our next meeting. We'd both be jolly dignified and pat each other on the back, and everything would end very pleasantly with a solemn handshake and condolences and congratulations all round. I was therefore a bit surprised when he burst through my door a few minutes later like one of those South Atlantic hurricanes Captain Spratt was so fond of describing over dinner.

'You swine!' He stood opening and closing his fists. 'You toad!'

'Ah, Basil, there you are! No hard feelings, I hope?'

'You stinking little sawbones! I've just been talking to Ophelia.'

I was a bit surprised at this, because, of course, she had a headache.

'And I fear she handed you your cards?' I observed sympathetically. 'Rotten for you, I admit. But at least you've awarded yourself a very nice consolation prize.' I gave a wink. 'As far as Ophelia's concerned, it's just another case of best man win, and all that, eh?'

I extended my hand.

Basil spat on it.

'Here, I say! This isn't quite the way to behave just because you've been unlucky in love.'

'You poisonous little pill pedlar!'

'I mean,' I went on with a little laugh, 'you may henceforward be frightfully lucky at cards.'

Basil advanced into the cabin.

'Will you stop that drivelling before I break your filthy neck?'

'Now, just a minute –' I started to feel annoyed with the idiot. 'You've no business to carry on like this simply because Ophelia has turned you into the snow. Why, if everybody created like you, the ruddy country would be like a gladiator's benefit night. Besides, now you've got your van Barn to keep you warm. Dash it!' I became rather indignant. 'You can't have your crumpet and eat it too. I might tell you, Basil, I am becoming a little weary of continually hearing about Ophelia and you –'

'Oh, damn Ophelia and me! It's Ophelia and *you* I'm concerned about.'

'I admit she's shown a slight preference –'

'It might interest you to know, you unholy sewer rat, that Ophelia has told me everything. Everything! Starting before Christmas.'

'Er, yes,' I said. In the excitement, I'd rather forgotten the train of events.

'She told me the lot. The absolute lot!' Basil stood over

me, breathing on my face like a blowlamp. 'All the time I was sweating my heart in that ghastly pantomime in Blackport – cavorting before audiences composed entirely of deaf mutes, living in digs that would be a disgrace to a refugee camp, eating all that beastly tripe and queuing in the rain for those horrible trams – while I was suffering to earn a little money to set up a home for my future wife, you – you emasculated Jack the Ripper – were taking advantage of my absence in a manner unspeakably loathsome between bitter enemies, not to mention old trusted friends –'

'I – I just thought she might be a little lonely,' I explained.

'Har!'

I edged towards the door of the hospital.

'And anyway, it was all perfectly innocent –'

'Innocent? Great God! You lured that sweet girl into your Mayfair flat at night and proceeded to rip her clothes off –'

'Now look here!' This was too much. 'I never did anything of the kind.'

'I demand – Have you or have you not seen Ophelia naked?'

'Of course I have! But that was purely –'

'Thank you. That is all I want to know.'

'Dash it! It's perfectly easily explained –'

'Cur,' hissed Basil.

'Basil, my dear chap, I'm sure we can sit down and talk the whole matter over –'

'Let me get at you.'

'Here, hold on!' I grabbed the hospital door handle. 'After all, we are gentlemen.'

'One of us is. The other, by God! is shortly going to be unrecognizable as anything.'

'And one of us,' I snapped, now really narked, 'doesn't break open the lock of our gas meter and swipe all our Gas Board's hard earned shillings. Or leave our digs by the drainpipe without paying our week's rent. Not to mention that our landlady's daughter –'

'You dreg! You pustule!'

I slipped quickly inside the hospital. But Basil, with an agility I suppose coming from all those trap-doors, managed to stick his foot in the jamb. I bolted towards the far door. He followed. Noticing the amputation set which had interested Ophelia, he made a grab for the muscle scalpel.

'"Turn, hell-hound, turn!"' cried Basil. '"Thou bloodier villain than terms can give thee out!"'

There didn't seem much point in arguing with him any longer, so I disappeared down the deck.

Naturally, one dislikes being conspicuous in public. But this is jolly difficult to avoid when you're being chased by a chap with a six-inch knife in his hand yelling bloody murder. The passengers finishing off the Gala Dance in the Veranda Bar understandably looked startled at this interruption of normal shipboard routine, but instead of trying to save my life by catching Basil with a deck-croquet mallet they all removed themselves from the theatre of operations as quickly as possible. I ran on. The only thought that occurred to me was its being six times round the deck to the mile, and wondering whether Basil or I were best over the distance.

'"Then yield thee, coward!"' Basil shouted behind me. '"Yield".'

I turned a corner, and ran into Captain Spratt and the Bos'n.

'What the devil – ! Hell's teeth! It's that steward again.'

I stopped. Basil stopped. He stood for a moment looking rather foolish.

'Drop that knife at once!' thundered Captain Spratt. 'Unless you want me personally to beat the daylights out of you. Doctor!'

'Sir?'

'Became violent, eh?'

'Yes, sir,' I panted. 'In the hospital. Had to run for my life.'

'Just like the woman at Teneriffe. Bos'n – clap that man in irons.'

'Here, I say!' Basil suddenly seemed to realize his part had got out of hand. 'You can't simply put me away in some sort of padded cell –'

'I can certainly assure you your cell won't be padded.' The Captain quickly took a pinch of snuff. 'Brandishing an offensive weapon is mutiny, and mutiny on the high seas is punishable by imprisonment for life. On our return to London you will be handed over to the police and – after, of course, the usual trial – locked up in one of Her Majesty's prisons for a considerable period of time. You may think yourself lucky Beauchamp. In earlier days I could have hanged you at sunrise tomorrow from the yardarm. Take him away.'

'But it's all a frightful mistake!' The Bos'n caught Basil in a full Nelson. 'Just ask the doctor here – he's one of my oldest friends –'

'Mad as a hatter,' nodded the Captain.

'But Gaston, dear chappie! I am, aren't I?'

'Raving, I suppose, Doctor?'

'Sad case, sir.'

'Gaston! Grim! Ever since those days in the dear old digs –'

'Never seen him before he came on board, of course,' I added.

'Gaston! I appeal to you –'

'Carry on, Bos'n,' said the Captain.

15

I was a cad again, of course. But I didn't care. At last I'd been cured of the cataracts which had smitten my eyes since Christmas.

Simply to get a bit of her own back on Basil, Ophelia had deliberately tipped out the story of our love-life and jolly near lost me my skin. It suddenly struck me what a shocking little vixen the woman was. I wondered why on earth I hadn't tumbled to it long before that frightful chase round the deck, when she'd rapidly changed in status from the light of my life to my *bête blonde*.

You can understand she found a pretty reserved welcome the next morning when she had the temerity to tap on the door of my cabin.

'Darling, you *do* look pale and wan,' she greeted me. 'Perhaps you're not very well?'

'Not through lack of exercise, I assure you,' I returned crisply.

'You mean last night, darling? I'm so sorry about it. Dreadfully. I'd no idea Basil would get so excited.'

'Excited? Damn it! There was nearly murder on the high seas.'

Ophelia gave a sigh. 'I can't understand why he was so annoyed. After all, Basil and I are nothing to each other any longer, are we?'

I snorted. 'At least the chap's securely shut up between the chain lockers and the paint store, and won't be able to go round murdering anyone else till we're safely home in London.'

'Poor Basil!' murmured Ophelia.

'He's only got what he jolly well deserved.'

'Poor dear Basil!'

'Poor dear Basil, indeed! What about poor dear me?' I

demanded. 'You might have come up this morning and found me in slices.'

'But it's so terrible! Thinking of Basil rotting in gaol.'

'Personally, the idea keeps me in fits.'

Ophelia gave a little quiver, and started to weep like a cloudburst at Old Trafford.

Of course, you need a heart like a kerbstone to remain unmoved by a woman's tears, particularly Ophelia's. After a minute or two I began to shuffle a bit, and said uneasily:

'I expect he's quite comfy, really. He gets regular grub and plenty of fags. And after sharing a cabin with twelve other stewards, it must be rather nice to be on your own for a change.'

'I just can't bear to think of him!' I offered a handkerchief. 'Dear Basil! Do you suppose there are rats in his cell? He was always so frightened of mice.'

I passed the duty-free cigarette tin, but she was weeping so much she quite ruined half of them.

'And Sybil's terribly upset, too,' Ophelia went on, blowing her nose.

'Sybil? You mean Sybil van Barn?'

'She's really a very sweet person, once you get to know her. We had a long cry together this morning.'

I was about to make some nasty remark about bitch eat bitch, but all this weeping was making me so rattled I felt it time to turn off the supply at the mains.

'Now look here, Ophelia,' I said, civilly enough. 'We mustn't worry too much about Basil. If I simply explain to the Captain the perfect truth that he's really a psychiatric case, the chap will suffer nothing worse than being paid off at Rio and going home in another ship as a D.B.S.'

'A D.B. what?'

'A Distressed British Seaman.'

'Not Basil! No, never!'

'But dash it, Ophelia!' The blasted chap had anyway been a distressed British actor long enough not to notice the difference. 'This routine happens quite often –'

Ophelia dried her eyes. 'I'm going up to talk to the Captain.'

'I shouldn't think that will do much good,' I told her.

'Not by the look on his face when he and Basil last met.'

'Well, we'll see.' She produced a compact to dab her nose. 'Poor, poor Basil!'

'Poor Basil!' I muttered, as she left. I gave a convenient cushion a kick. Not only was the woman a first-class harpy, but, what was worse, she was absolutely ruddy impossible as well.

With Ophelia and Basil out of my life, there was nothing to occupy the vacant space except Sir Lancelot's memoirs. As we were getting on for Rio de Janeiro and the ventilating system kept breaking down the ship was pretty cosy, but I sat with a towel round my waist ploughing through stacks of after-dinner speeches the old boy had made years ago, which I hoped sounded better when you were leaning back after six courses with a cigar and brandy.

But as the day went by I couldn't help growing sorry for old Basil, sweating it out down below next to the paint. I supposed he wasn't a bad cove at heart. His only snag was the occupational disease of forever acting. During our little run round the deck, of course, he wasn't really Basil Beauchamp chasing Gaston Grimsdyke with an operating knife. He was Macduff after Macbeth all over Dunsinane. So a couple of mornings before we were due to arrive I pushed Sir Lancelot's life aside, slipped into my white uniform, and stepped on deck with the idea of bribing one of his guards to send him in a nice cold bottle of beer.

I turned the corner of the fan-house and tripped over the chap himself, stretched on a steamer chair dressed in purple bathing-trunks and holding a large gin and tonic.

'Basil!' I exclaimed. 'But my dear old lad! You've escaped.'

He returned the greeting with a long blank stare.

'But damn it!' I demanded. 'What on earth are you doing, lounging about in the sun with the first-class passengers?'

'I happen to *be* a first-class passenger, thank you,' he replied coldly.

I wondered for a moment if all his nasty experiences had really unhinged him.

Basil took a puff of the cigar he happened to be smoking.

'Do I gather from your epaulettes you are the ship's doctor?'

'Of course I'm the ship's doctor, you idiot. You know jolly well –'

'Then kindly remember your position as a member of the crew.'

'Now look here.' I glanced round. 'A lark's a lark, but I wish you'd chuck playing the travelling milord and explain it. Besides, if old Shuttleworth comes and catches you –'

'I don't understand, Doctor.' Basil looked me up and down. 'Indeed, I don't even recall seeing you before today.'

'Basil, you fool! Why, even in the old digs –'

'Mr Beauchamp, if you please. Nip across to the bar and fetch me another gin and tonic, will you?'

'You get your own ruddy gin and tonics.'

Basil sighed. 'Dear me, the insubordination of the crew. I really must write to the Company about it.'

'Why the hell,' I demanded, 'aren't you this very moment picking oakum in the bilges?'

Basil slowly finished his drink. 'I have a very good friend on board – a Miss Ophelia O'Brien. Perhaps you know her? She acquainted Captain Spratt with certain facts concerning my presence in the ship, and prevailed on the dear old gentleman to effect my release. After a few formalities before our consul in Rio, I shall be released from my contract with the shipping company. There being no option clause, I am then free to return to my native land.'

'Yes, sweating it out as a D.B.S. among the coffee beans in a beastly tramp.'

'Another good friend on board – a Mrs van Barn,' Basil went on calmly, 'has prevailed on the Captain to accept my first-class fare for the rest of the voyage. She is also most kindly defraying my expenses to London. We shall be travelling together, via New York. I shall be staying at the Waldorf. By the way, Doctor – I may be needing some extensive medical treatment on board for my nerves. I shall probably summon you to my cabin at odd intervals during the afternoon, so don't bother to lie down for your customary nap, will you?'

We arrived at Rio de Janeiro.

Ophelia flew home to London. I didn't bother to say good-bye to her. Basil flew with Mrs van Barn to New York, and I didn't expect him to bother to say good-bye to me, anyway. I was left leaning on the rail, thinking about life.

'Doctor!'

I turned as Captain Spratt appeared.

'Sir?'

'Doctor, I have a matter of some seriousness to raise with you,' he began. 'Mr Shuttleworth has reported that on one occasion during the voyage you were seen in the Veranda Bar not only drinking *crème de menthe,* but actually holding the hand of a young lady passenger, who shall go nameless. You know perfectly well my views on that sort of thing. You are absolutely without excuse. I have no alternative whatever but to suspend your shore leave in Rio de Janeiro, and forbid you from drinking at all or appearing on the passenger decks for the remainder of the voyage. Good afternoon.'

16

'I trust you had a pleasant holiday in the company of my young brother George,' said Sir Lancelot Spratt. 'No doubt the rest and tranquillity traditionally associated with ocean voyages has done you the world of good.'

As I'd just taken my first pint for three weeks, and my first step on land for six, I didn't know what to reply.

'I happened to hear at a City dinner the other week that he had been obliged to find his sea-legs again.' The surgeon paused, standing before the fire. 'It is perhaps sometimes difficult fully to appreciate the company of my brother.'

I agreed heartily myself.

'He has this nauseating habit of cramming his cranial sinuses with snuff. I warned him years ago it would play the very devil with his mucous membrane, but it wasn't the slightest use.' Sir Lancelot snapped open his gold watch. 'I see it is six o'clock. Perhaps you would join me in a glass of sherry?'

He touched a bell beside the fireplace.

I'd gone straight to his Harley Street home to report progress of the memoirs, which had occupied my sober attention all the way home from Rio. I'd got on rather well with them, the only compensation for a voyage which I personally thought the greatest maritime disaster since the *Titanic*.

'I am particularly pleased you have returned at this precise moment, Grimsdyke,' continued Sir Lancelot. 'Because I am anxious for you to witness – and naturally to record in the book – an event imminent in my life which, in its way, may prove its crowning achievement.'

I sat up. 'Good Lord, sir, you're not being ennobled?'

'On the contrary, I am being sued.'

I looked puzzled. I'd had a few nasty letters from tailors' solicitors and the like in my time, and this didn't strike me as much of a feat.

'It is a depressing sign of the age,' Sir Lancelot went on regretfully. 'Patients aren't grateful any more. In the old days you could half kill a man, and he'd still send you a box of cigars for Christmas. Now they've no sooner finished their free treatment in hospital than they're round the corner getting free legal aid and sue the doctor. But I suppose we can expect nothing less, with the monstrous remarks that are being made in the courts. You've seen the morning's *Times*?'

I nodded, a bunch of newspapers having appeared with the Thames pilot.

'You mean the case of some unfortunate doctor getting it in the neck for professional negligence, sir?'

'Exactly.' Sir Lancelot hitched up his coat. 'That a judge, who knows nothing whatever about medicine except what he reads in the bed-time drink advertisements in the newspapers, can have the temerity to instruct us in public how to perform our own job, is to my mind a gross abuse of constitutional authority.'

He rang the bell again.

I tried hard to remember something particularly juicy the beak had said, but could recall only a few remarks about doctors never telling patients what's wrong with them, which, of course, is perfectly true, anyway.

'I suppose learned judges rather get into the habit of laying down the law, sir.'

'Mr Justice Fishwick is about as learned as my left femur. I roomed with the feller when he was reading for the Bar, and he was always coming down to cadge cigarettes and blotting-paper. Weedy little man with nasty teeth, and everything he ate brought him out in rather unpleasant rashes. Now I come to think of it, he borrowed my fountain-pen for the Bar finals, and as far as I remember never returned it.'

Sir Lancelot gave the bell another push.

'I would write to *The Times* myself,' he added, 'except that it is one of my principles never to write letters to the newspapers. It is in the worst possible taste to inflict your opinions on total strangers over breakfast. Besides, you never get paid for them.'

Sir Lancelot then opened the drawing-room door and called 'Maria!' several times in a loud voice.

'What on earth's all that commotion?' demanded his wife outside.

'I am merely requesting a glass of sherry for myself and my guest, my dear.' He shouted 'Maria!' a bit more. 'Where the devil has the girl got to?'

'Why, good evening, Gaston.' Lady Spratt appeared. 'We don't seem to have seen you for quite a time. Have you been away? It won't do the slightest good shouting like that, Lancelot. Maria has left.'

'Left?' Sir Lancelot looked insulted. 'What do you mean, "Left"? I thought she was so happy with us?'

'And I expect she will be even happier with the American airman she's going to marry.'

'But damnation! Who's going to look after the house? Surely you've engaged someone else?'

'Please remember, dear, this is your home and not your hospital. You cannot simply clap your hands and get someone running to do all the dirty work.'

'Really, Maud! You should have informed me first –'

'Don't get so excited, dear. Of course I've asked the agency to send another girl. Meanwhile, if you want the sherry you'll find it on the dining-room sideboard as usual.'

'When this legal affair started I didn't know if it were laughable or contemptible,' continued Sir Lancelot, reappearing with a decanter and glasses. 'My first instinct was to ignore the whole business, but your cousin Miles kept nagging me to see my solicitors. He has become rather sanctimonious since joining this Immorality Commission. "The peculiar repulsiveness of those who dabble their fingers self-approvingly in the stuff of other's souls",' he growled. 'You know your Virginia Woolf? Have some sherry.'

'Perhaps the case will never come to court, sir,' I

suggested to cheer them up. 'I gather a good many never get beyond the slanging stage.'

'Preposterous as it may seem, it *is* coming to court. Just as I was congratulating myself on keeping clear of the legal fraternity, since all that fuss over the idiotic magistrate who thought I'd parked on the wrong side of Harley Street. Though how any judge with more than half his wits and less than half asleep can possibly fail to throw my case straight out again is totally beyond my comprehension.'

I must say I felt a little cagey over this, having once had no end of trouble about some errand boy who rode his bicycle under my Bentley. But I supposed at least they couldn't send the old boy to clink, or even endorse his licence.

Lady Spratt reached for a cigarette. 'Did you hear any more from the Medical Legal Insurance, dear?'

Sir Lancelot grunted. 'All I got out of that lily-livered bunch were orders to settle out of court. However, I insist on fighting the case and risking the costs from my own pocket. I shall, of course, be represented by my elder brother, who will cut down somewhat on the expenses.'

'Your elder brother?' I looked surprised.

'Yes, he has made quite a thing of it at the Bar.'

I'd often read in the papers of Mr Alphonso Spratt, Q.C., who was always appearing in complicated cases arising from City wizards doing the dirty on each other. I supposed he was the one referred to briefly in Sir Lancelot's papers as 'Ugly Alfie'.

'You will kindly attend a conference on the case in my brother's chambers in the Temple on Wednesday afternoon at three, Grimsdyke. We can meet just beforehand at my solicitors'. I wish you to document most carefully every word of these proceedings. They will not only, of course, provide me with total vindication. They may well have the same importance for our profession as the case of John Hampden and the ship-money for our nation.' He swallowed his sherry. 'Where are you staying in Town? I'm afraid it is quite impossible for me to put you up, in view of our domestic disorganization.'

'I'm lodging for a bit with Miles, sir.'

'We'd love to have you,' agreed Lady Spratt. 'But I'm afraid one guest is as much as we can manage just now.'

Sir Lancelot looked up. 'Guest? What guest?'

'Didn't I tell you, dear? My brother will be arriving this evening. You know how he has to come up to London, now he's Chairman of the Royal Commission.'

Sir Lancelot kicked the fender. 'Maud, this is absolutely outrageous! Good God! These Royal Commissions sit for ever, and I'll be dead and buried for years before you get the blasted fellow out of the house. Even fully staffed life becomes utterly impossible in his presence –'

'Lancelot, there's really no need to become so dramatic.'

'I'll tell you what I'll do. I'm perfectly prepared to put the fellow up at the Savoy at my own expense –'

'You know that's out of the question. Besides, he must have his home comforts.'

'My home comforts, you mean.'

Sir Lancelot turned pink. I must say, I could sympathize with the old boy. After all that trouble to free the house of bishops, here they were creeping back again with the warmer weather.

'I suppose this time he's coming alone?' he asked shortly. 'I know how I'll tackle the feller. I shall render him a bill every Saturday morning for professional advice tendered during the week.' He paused, breathing heavily. 'I think, Grimsdyke, you had better leave us. I wish to go to my study and sit for a moment in peace, while that is still possible.'

I said good-bye, strolled up the Marylebone Road, and took a bus across London to Miles' house in South Kensington. And a pretty thoughtful sixpennyworth it was, too.

It was all very fine and large Sir Lancelot roping me in for his court case, but knowing the legal boys regarded time the same way as the Spanish peasants, I felt it might take months sorting out. And here I was going about with the great novel busting inside me, like a new tube of toothpaste. Besides, I couldn't sponge on Miles for ever, and the episode of Ophelia had left me suffering acutely from the old complaint of anaemia of the exchequer. In fact, I reckoned as we turned Hyde Park Corner, if I didn't buckle to the new book soon for my fresh bunch of publishers, I should be facing poverty – the real grinding stuff. But I remembered if it hadn't been for Sir Lancelot removing my appendix I should have been some mute inglorious Grimsdyke, and a fat lot of good that would have done anybody.

Miles hit on the same problem in his own little way as he stood me a whisky and soda that night before I retired, rather looking forward to his spare bed instead of the cradle of the deep.

'After that unfortunate experience with your publishers, Gaston,' he remarked, 'I wonder you don't abandon this adventure of novel writing for good. Why can't you simply return to the serious practice of medicine?'

'That might be difficult,' I hedged. 'I mean, you wouldn't open an abdomen with a rusty scalpel.'

'I could easily arrange a refresher course with my own students at St Swithin's.'

'But as old Trollope put it, "It is difficult for a man to go back to the verdure and malleability of pupildom, who has once escaped from the necessary humility of its conditions." '

This seemed to floor him for a bit, then he went on, 'I don't want to seem at all uncharitable your first night home in England, but I will make no secret of its being a great relief to me if you settled in a more orderly way of life. I will be frank. Any other existence might reflect on my position as a Royal Commissioner. The honour has come to me unexpectedly early – admittedly I have published many useful papers on moral problems – and you know how I wish to make a success of it.'

The same dear old Miles, I thought, always expecting everybody to stop what they were doing and attend to his own little problems first. It was just the same at school, whenever anyone pinched his marbles.

'I'll give it some thought,' I promised, helping myself to another whisky. 'Meanwhile,' I asked, to get off the subject, 'perhaps you can give me the low-down on how the law and Sir Lancelot collided?'

It had all started in Sir Lancelot's Thursday morning Out-patients', which at St Swithin's is a ceremony rather than a clinic. The affair is held in a long room with white-tiled walls, which strike you as cold and formal as an old-fashioned boiled shirt-front. At one end is the consultant's desk with a big brass inkpot and one of those little bells you use to call the barmaid in country pubs. At the other is a laboratory bench with a Bunsen burner, and a black-board for Sir Lancelot to draw interesting bits of people's insides in coloured chalks. The space between is filled with rows of wooden benches apparently bought second-hand from railway stations, on which the chaps crowd to watch the niceties.

That morning Sir Lancelot appeared as usual, the buzz of conversation stopping like a swatted fly.

'Mr Harris.'

He fixed his eye on the nearest student.

'Sir?'

'Where can we discover a classical case of under-functioning of the pituitary gland?'

The student quaked a bit, naturally.

'The endocrine clinic, sir?'

'The public library. The Fat Boy in *Pickwick Papers* presents all the clinical features, though neither Dickens nor anyone else at the time had ever heard the slightest mention of the endocrine glands. Observation, ladies and gentlemen! That is ninety per cent of medicine. The other ten per cent is common sense. So you may console yourselves that lack of brains is no bar to professional advancement. The first patient, Sister, if you please.'

The Out-patient sisters usher them in and out with the practised briskness of Old Bailey wardresses, and the first that morning was a woman with gallstones, which Sir Lancelot drew several feet across on the blackboard.

'Cholelithiasis, madam, a long Greek word which won't convey anything to you in the slightest,' he explained as usual, when she had the temerity to ask what was the matter with her. The old boy regarded any patient asking the diagnosis as taking a morbid interest in themselves. 'So don't worry your head about it – I'm the one who does the worrying from now on, and there's nothing for you to bother about except doing exactly what I tell you and getting better. Next patient, please.'

A weedy chap in a blue suit appeared, clutching a bowler hat.

'Mr Harris, what do you observe?' Sir Lancelot demanded. 'Why, the boots, man, the boots! Note the worn inner surface – a clear case of flat feet. How long have you suffered from this distressing condition, my good man?'

'Sir Lancelot Spratt?'

'I believe that is the name displayed on the door.'

'I have this for you, sir.'

Whipping a paper from his hat, the chap slipped it into the surgeon's top pocket and made flat-footedly for the door.

Everyone gasped. There hadn't been such a sensation in the place since Sir Lancelot set his trousers alight with the Bunsen.

'Sister!' he roared. 'Can't you keep a closer eye on the patients? That fellow is raving mad. He could easily have assassinated me if he'd had a pistol hidden in his hat. As it happens, he has contented himself with presenting me with some sort of tract –'

It was then he noticed the paper was covered with nasty phrases in gothic writing like 'High Court of Justice' and 'We command You.'

'But I'm afraid he only tossed it aside, muttering something about tomfoolery,' ended Miles sadly. 'In fact, his only response was making the rest of the patients strip naked and come up wrapped in the surgery bath-towel.'

17

I'd never mixed much with lawyers, except when fixing the St Swithin's *v.* Inns of Court rugger matches in the 'Bell and Bottle' behind the Law Courts, where you find them by the dozen downing the beer and sandwiches in their black coats and striped trousers. Come to think of it, it's one of the charming conveniences of London that you can hobnob with any profession if you happen to know the right pub – you find doctors in the 'White Hart' opposite Barts, stockbrokers elbowing each other in the 'George and Vulture' on Cornhill, M.P.s knocking it back at the 'St Stephen's' in Westminster, artists in the 'Cross Keys' at Chelsea, and even professional Marxists telling funny stories to each other in the 'Nag's Head' near the Communist headquarters in Covent Garden.

From Sir Lancelot's remarks over the years I'd expected his solicitors to lurk in a Dickensian garret up among the chimneys of Cheapside, and was therefore rather surprised to find one of those modern buildings all made of windows, with slim-legged office furniture and secretaries to match. The solicitor himself, far from adding up to both Dodson and Fogg, was a youngish bird quite as smartly turned out as any car salesman in Piccadilly.

'Sorry I'm late, Beckwith,' grunted Sir Lancelot as he bustled in.

He was in a pretty black mood, I gathered from having to boil his own breakfast egg and the Bishop nabbing *The Times*.

'Now let us make haste to dispose of this totally preposterous situation.' Sir Lancelot came briskly to business. 'It is not only outrageous but somewhat insulting for anyone to suggest that *I* have committed professional negligence. I can assure you, Beckwith, that I have never been negligent in my life, except over remembering my blasted wedding anniversary. I am not at all certain that I haven't a case for litigation against these people myself for gross defamation of character.'

'Everyone's suing their surgeon these days,' smiled Beckwith, with the cosily reassuring air of a good family doctor. 'There's quite an epidemic, in fact.'

'An epidemic which I fully intend to stamp out. I have no doubt whatever that the result of this case will provide an excellent remedy.'

'Anyway, there's no need to worry about it, Sir Lancelot. Any worrying from now on can be safely left to us.'

'Let me assure you that I am not worrying in the slightest. I merely want to know from you, Beckwith, my precise legal position.'

The solicitor pursued his lips. 'That would involve a lot of lawyer's jargon which wouldn't mean anything to you, I'm afraid. And now,' he added, in the more businesslike tone of a good family doctor telling you to start taking your clothes off. 'I think it's time we were making for your brother's chambers.'

Mr Alphonso Spratt provided a more legal atmosphere, all mahogany and leather bindings and no open windows, with seedy-looking old boys poking about among piles of papers done up with red tape.

'Where's Alfie?' muttered Sir Lancelot as we entered.

'Good afternoon, Mr Beckwith. I'm afraid that Mr Spratt has been delayed,' said one of the seedy birds, fussing up.

'I am a very busy man,' Sir Lancelot told him.

'And so is Mr Spratt,' replied the seedy bird, showing us into an inner office.

'Alfie always was an untidy hound,' grunted Sir Lancelot, glancing round more piles of paper. 'His bedroom was an absolute disgrace.'

As we sat down, he went on, 'Thank God I haven't been exposed to this nefarious part of the world since the days when I used to give medical evidence for Hoppings. Remember him, Beckwith? He specialized in elderly gentlemen behaving peculiarly in Hyde Park. Then they improved the Park lighting and he lost his practice.'

Sir Lancelot spent the next five minutes glaring at an etching of a severe-looking chap in a large wig, whom I fancied was Judge Jeffreys. Suddenly the door burst open, and Mr Alphonso Spratt shot in.

'My dear Lancelot! How extraordinarily pleasant to see you.'

He was thinner than the surgeon, his beard was greyer, his hair was longer, and his voice was fruitier.

'So sorry I'm a trifle late,' he apologized briefly. 'At this very moment I should be on my feet in the Court of Appeal.'

'And at this very moment,' said Sir Lancelot, shaking hands coldly, 'I should be on my feet in my operating theatre.'

Alphonso didn't seem to notice this remark, but settling in the most comfortable chair went on briskly, 'Let's get this little matter straight in our minds, shall we?'

He produced a crocodile case from an inside pocket and lit a cigar.

'This young man is my amanuensis,' explained Sir Lancelot, as his brother gave me a curious glance. 'Now look here, Alfie, I want you to understand from the start the importance of this action. The point is not simply to justify myself, but the entire practice of British surgery. I cannot put it too strongly. Personally, I was about to chuck the original communication from these impossible people into the wastepaper basket –'

'Good Heavens, that was a High Court writ, not a bookie's circular,' muttered Alphonso, looking shocked.

Beckwith handed him a bundle of papers.

'But hadn't you been getting letters from their solicitors?' asked the barrister, looking a bit puzzled.

'Of course I had, man! For months.'

'Then where, may I ask, have they got to?'

'Naturally I tore them up. You cannot expect someone with my volume of work to fritter away valuable time with a lot of litigious lunatics. I was finally persuaded to consult Beckwith here. Unlike the rest of the population, I fortunately do not regard money spent on professional advice as wasted. Though the whole business is, of course, as ridiculous as Gilbert and Sullivan.'

Alphonso puffed his cigar. 'On the contrary, I must advise you to take it with the utmost seriousness.'

Sir Lancelot looked startled. 'But damnation! It's just a piece of dastardly blackmail.'

'Most court cases are, of course,' his brother returned calmly. 'Now let's see – who's this Herbert Egbert Thomas Possett?'

'An extremely stupid young man with a duodenal ulcer, which he perforated at an unusually early age, and which I repaired perfectly competently in St Swithin's, Sir Lancelot explained. 'He also has a mother, who made a frightful nuisance of herself in the ward. I believe them both to be a little touched.'

'Indeed?' Alphonso looked up. 'Perhaps you could obtain the written opinion of a psychiatrist?'

'Damn it, Alfie! It's not the slightest use bringing in psychiatrists, or water-diviners or spiritualists, if it comes to that. If I say a man's mad, he's mad, and that's all there is to it. Surely you're not suggesting that anyone could doubt my opinions?'

'But he says here in his statement of claim you should never have operated on him at all.'

'I can tell you here and now that if I hadn't operated on the ungrateful idiot, I ought to have been hanged, not sued.'

'Dear me,' said Alphonso. He took a monocle from his waistcoat pocket and started shifting the papers.

'Possett complains that since the operation he's suffered from pains in the stomach and blackouts,' he observed after a bit.

'So do half the population,' replied Sir Lancelot shortly. 'Will you please understand, Alfie, that you needn't bother your head about the obvious medical facts? You just leave all that to me. Your job is simply to put this fellow in his place. Then I assure you I shall be perfectly prepared to forget the whole affair.'

He made a generous sweep of his hand, knocking over the solicitor's brief-case.

'Mr Beckwith,' said Alphonso, who seemed to be tiring rather quickly of his brother's company. 'Is this a case of *res ipsa loquitur*?'

'I hardly think so.'

He tapped the ash from his cigar. 'Then it's not on all fours with *Polkinghorne v. Ministry of Health*?'

'I feel more likely with *Stumley v. Typhoon Feather Pluckers*.'

The barrister screwed in his monocle. 'But that surely brings us against *Heaviside v. Kiddiwinks Toys, Bournemouth Aquarium Intervening*?'

'Forgive me, Alfie,' interrupted Sir Lancelot, 'but would you kindly tell me what the devil you two are talking about?'

'My dear fellow, I'm afraid it wouldn't convey anything in the slightest to you if I did. Just leave the worrying to me, there's a good chap. You content yourself with following my instructions, then I'll win your case.'

Sir Lancelot glared. 'You are surely not suggesting for one second that you won't?'

'Not at all. Indeed, I will go so far as saying your chances are not unreasonable – '

'No unreasonable!' Sir Lancelot thumped the table, raising quite a cloud of dust. 'But damn it, Alfie! Any fool could tell this Possett's a screaming neurotic. All these symptoms he's making a song and dance about are totally hysterical and imaginary. There should be some sort of law against things like this ever coming into court.'

'I suppose you haven't seriously considered the possibility of settling?'

'Settling?' Sir Lancelot jumped to his feet. 'Kindly get this clear, Alfie. I will not lie down and have my rights trampled upon, and I'm damned proud of it. It was exactly the same over that parking summons, when I refused to be dictated to by some inflated greengrocer perched on a magistrate's bench – '

'I would not be disinclined to advise a settlement.'

'Indeed?' thundered Sir Lancelot. 'I suppose you advise all your blackmailed clients simply to pay up and say nothing?'

'I do not handle criminal business,' replied his brother crisply.

'Settle! By God! Fine fools we'd be to settle, when the case will be laughed into the street –'

'I myself would certainly hesitate to say what might happen to any case whatever in court.' Alphonso glared through his monocle. 'You seem extremely disinclined to accept my opinion on anything, Lancelot. But you might at least take my advice that judges are like horses, and liable to jump in perfectly unexpected directions.'

'But Alfie, you fool! Surely you cannot for one instant believe a word of this fantastic accusation?'

'My own opinions are unfortunately entirely without importance in the matter.'

'Alfie, you're a blackguard.'

Mr Alphonso Spratt dropped his monocle.

'Damn you, Lancelot! Have you no respect for the law?'

'I have the utmost respect for the law. But I have no respect whatever for lawyers. As it is quite obvious that my presence here is totally unnecessary, I shall return to my hospital and perform some useful work. Come, Grimsdyke. Good afternoon.'

We left. The seedy-looking chaps listening outside looked like the passengers in the Veranda Bar when I appeared with Basil.

'I fancy Sir Lancelot didn't like it much being the patient for a change,' I suggested, describing all this to Miles over a whisky and soda that night.

My cousin made a little impatient noise.

'I do wish he would be sensible and let himself be persuaded to settle the matter out of court. He doesn't give a thought to the most damaging effect of the publicity on St Swithin's.'

I agreed. 'Always a pretty nasty business, washing dirty hospital linen in public.'

'Not to mention risking a severe financial loss. And there would be little chance of our seeing him as next President of the Royal College of Surgeons.'

I agreed with that, too. If Sir Lancelot lost his case, making him a President would be like promoting a Captain who'd just lost his ship.

'Besides,' continued Miles moodily, 'he never considers for a moment how the affair might reflect on myself. I must be extremely circumspect these days. Not to mention our most worthy Chairman, the Bishop of Wincanton. I believe you've met him. A charming man. It's remarkable how active he remains in spite of such indifferent health. Being under the same roof, he finds Sir Lancelot's behaviour at times most upsetting.

'I made a rather interesting calculation today,' Miles went on. 'Do you realize in the few nights you have spent here, you have consumed quite two-thirds of a bottle of whisky?' He gave a dry little laugh. 'I shall have to add it to your weekly bill.'

I gave a dry little laugh, too.

'Quite a joke, Gaston, if I presented you with an account for board and lodging every Friday?'

'As a matter of fact, old lad,' I told him, 'I was planning to leave tomorrow morning.'

I wasn't, of course, but it's remarkable how sensitive I am even to the subtlest of hints.

'Stay as long as you wish, naturally,' added Miles quickly, looking greatly relieved. 'We are all delighted to have you, particularly young Bartholomew. Though what exactly,' he asked after a pause, 'are you intending to do?'

'Take a quiet room, finish Sir Lancelot's memoirs, and start my new novel.' I reached for one of his cigarettes. 'Which rather brings me to the point. You know under the old grandpa's will, just before he was eaten by that tiger, he left you some cash for me when I reached a highly mature age? I just wondered if you'd mind slipping across a little on account.'

'I'm afraid that's completely out of the question.'

'But dash it! It's just to pay the rent and grocery bills while I do the novel for this new lot of publishers.'

Miles gave one of the looks I suppose he used frequently on the Royal Commission.

'Please do not think me censorious, but I feel it would more likely be dissipated on the entertainment of some young woman.'

'That's a jolly unsporting accusation – '

'Not in the least. Will you kindly recall your last visit here, at Christmas? You then confessed yourself seriously in love with a lady whom you wished to marry. I don't seem to have heard you mention the project since.'

'Ah, yes,' I said. Odd how quickly one forgets such things. 'It was simply that I made a slight mistake in the diagnosis.'

'Then I certainly don't intend encouraging you to make similar ones. You may rest assured that if you ever do marry a suitable girl I shall advance you the money – at the conclusion of the ceremony Meanwhile, you should be delighted to know you have such a nest-egg.'

'Which will be pretty addled by the time I have my hands on it,' I told him shortly.

Knowing that getting cash out of Miles was like trying to get blood out of a thrombosed varicose vein, I was prepared to let the subject drop. But he went on:

'I do implore you to take up serious medical work again instead of this stupid novel writing. You know I could easily arrange for you to have a resident post at the Tooting Temperance Hospital –'

'My dear old lad! When will you get it into your head that I'm really not cut out to be a doctor?'

'But damnation, Gaston! The waste of your education –'

'Not at all.' I eyed him a bit. 'Somerset Maugham said he couldn't imagine better training for a writer than a few years in the medical profession. And he ought to know. After all, he's a doctor, too.'

Miles snorted. 'To my mind they should pass a law to erase non-practising physicians from the *Medical Register*.'

'Some hope of that,' I told him. 'The House of Commons is full of them.'

After that he stood up and bad-temperedly announced he was going to bed. I stayed behind, and just for the fun of it finished the rest of his bottle of whisky.

18

'Dr Grimsdyke,' announced the pretty little receptionist, 'that man's behaving strangely in the waiting-room again.'

'Good Lord!' I looked up from the doctors' motoring column in the *British Medical Journal*. 'Surely not the one with the faces – ?'

She nodded. 'I'm afraid he's getting worse. This time he seems to be making love to his hat.'

I rose briskly from the Chippendale consulting desk.

'Oh, he is, is he? Right! You just show the perisher inside. No, wait a minute – hide the scalpels from the suture tray first.'

It was a couple of months later, spring had been switched on, the parks were lightly covered with bright new flowers and the girls lightly covered with bright new dresses, and I was back in Razzy Potter-Phipps' Mayfair consulting-room again.

It had been a pretty miserable couple of months, too, since that row with Miles, when I'd moved into a beastly basement somewhere in Paddington. I hadn't expected to hear any more of Sir Lancelot's case for a bit, knowing how the wheels of the law make the works in a grandfather clock look like an Aston Martin gearbox, so I'd settled down at last to start the great novel.

But writing a novel, like setting a fracture, is rather more tricky than appears from the finished result. Whether it was the subterranean atmosphere, the filthy weather we were having, the after-effects of Sir Lancelot's massed speeches, or all the trains fussing about across the road, I never seemed to get further than fiddling with those interesting little screws they stick here and there over typewriters. Acute poverty set in. I put the grandpa's cuff-links up the spout, having long ago flogged the dear old

1930 Bentley. If the wolf kept from the door, it was only because of a pretty unappetizing Grimsdyke reared on baked beans and weak tea inside. I was tempted more than once to invite myself round to Miles' for a meal, top it off with a portion of humble pie, and take that job in Tooting. But I resisted. I remembered that Dostoyevsky only really struck form after five years in Siberia.

Taking a stroll to raise my spirits and vitamin-D level in the first April sunshine, I'd noticed it glinting on Razzy's town Jaguar parked outside a block of flats in Berkeley Square. A moment later the chap came hurrying out himself, followed by a chauffeur carrying the special vibrator he used for shaking up sluggish millionaires.

'Dear boy, what a stroke of luck!' Razzy exclaimed at once. 'I thought you were miles and miles away on the high seas. And how wonderfully slim you look! I really must try and take off some weight myself. Cigarette?'

I accepted gratefully.

'I suppose,' he added, after a bit of chat about the prospects for the racing season, 'you couldn't possibly find time to hold the fort for me on odd afternoons, could you?'

I looked doubtful. 'I'm getting a bit rusty for any serious medicine –'

'Dear boy, it isn't the medicine in my practice that's serious. After all, you can always call in a specialist for *that* sort of thing. It's the patients who are the worry. Perhaps you've noticed in the press about this Italian *prima donna* I've been treating for temperamental nervousness?'

I nodded. 'You mean, you want the afternoons free to nip round to Covent Garden and soothe her down before the performance?'

Razzy gave a cough. 'It isn't quite that, dear boy. In point of fact, it's simpler all round to attend to her case after the show at night. But I'm afraid ... well, the treatment seems to be taking such a terrible lot out of *me*, I really could do with a few hours' rest and recuperation between whiles. Do you ... do you think that you could possibly start straight away this afternoon?' he ended anxiously.

So I moved back to Park Lane, and jolly pleasant it was

too, particularly as Razzy threw in lunch. And now my peace was disturbed by the flutter of chickens coming home to roost.

'My dear chappie!' Basil stood in the consulting room doorway with a great idiotic grin on his face. 'You've got your old part back.'

'Good afternoon, Beauchamp.' My tone indicated that the milk of human kindness was in the deep freeze.

'What a delightful surprise!'

He seemed fairly bursting at the waistcoat buttons with affability. It's always the same with actors, spitting venom at you one minute and terrific pals the next, just like Miles' young Bartholomew.

'But I've been wondering how to get in touch with you for simply weeks, Grim.'

'Kindly be seated, Beauchamp.'

I wondered if I'd have the luck to give him an injection with one of those needles Razzy kept for customers getting behind with their bills.

'And what's the trouble this time?' I demanded shortly.

'I should like a complete medical examination, please. You see, dear chappie, I am shortly going to be married.'

'What again? You mean to –'

'To a charming widow called Sybil van Barn. But you've met, of course.'

'You don't mean to tell me you're actually going to marry that old –'

Basil offered a gold cigarette case.

'I will admit to you, dear chappie, some slight disparity in age and marital experience. But "Let me not to the marriage of true minds Admit impediments." After all, what is the most important thing to be fully shared between husband and wife? A common interest, naturally.' Basil flicked a lighter with his initials on it in rubies. 'And Sybil is tremendously interested in the stage. Yes, indeed. Did you know that the first of her defunct husbands owned all the theatres down one side of Broadway? And her second all the ones down the other?'

I snorted. 'A pity she didn't get to know Barnum and Bailey as well.'

'So you can understand, dear chappie, how glad I am that I tore myself away from London to take that cruise.' Basil twitched his new flannel trousers. 'An awful bore at the time, of course. But how worth it to find someone like Sybil at the same table.'

That idiot Basil, I thought, running true to form. He'd quite forgotten he came aboard as Steward Beauchamp, and a pretty rotten one at that.

'My fiancée is arriving from New York next week, and we shall be married in June. St George's, Hanover Square. You'll be invited, naturally. We've bought one of those charming little manors in Sussex, which are photographed for the American magazines to tempt tourists into our horrible hotels. Sybil's terribly keen on the real English background, and at week-ends I shall be able to indulge my fondness for country pursuits –'

'So far confined to raising pansies in a box outside your window in the digs.'

Basil adjusted his new pearl tie-pin.

'You can imagine how frightfully busy I am just now arranging everything, not to mention handling all these theatrical managers and film producers who do so keep pestering one. You've heard I'm opening as Hamlet this season? Sybil wants to stage an entirely new conception of the Gloomy Dane –'

'Popping through trap doors, I suppose?' I asked.

Basil looked hurt.

'Do I detect, dear chappie,' he demanded, 'a certain reserve in your manner this afternoon?'

'Yes, you jolly well do. You have the cheek to come barging in here putting on no end of airs, when it wasn't long since you were cadging bobs off me to cook your Sunday kipper over the gas ring. Not to mention recently trying to dissect me on the hoof.'

Basil sighed. 'Our little rift, dear Grim, has been quite troubling me. On the ship I was quite unable to sleep at night.'

'So I noticed. You kept getting me out of bed for sedatives.'

'But *All's Well That Ends Well.*'

'It may have done for you, but what ruddy well about me? As far as I'm concerned, it's *Love's Labour's Lost.*'

'Dear chappie!' He put out his newly manicured hand. 'I do so want us to be chums again.'

I hesitated.

'Please, Grim! Remember the dear old digs.'

I thought again. After all, I'd been rather a cad towards him. Though I bet there's not many chaps who could face their Recording Angels – not to mention their wives and their Income Tax Collectors – without admitting they'd been rather a cad regularly twice a week since the age of sixteen.

'Oh, all right then,' I said.

'I'm so glad,' smiled Basil. 'Because there is a certain little matter that can only be discussed in a most friendly way.' He had a smell at his carnation. 'I've recently been thinking a good deal about little Ophelia.'

As a matter of fact, I had too. It was difficult to avoid it, as you saw her every time you travelled by Underground, leaping about in the latest in girdles.

'An exceptional girl,' added Basil. 'Nature hasn't provided many such creatures.'

I agreed. Nature hasn't provided many female panthers, either, but you didn't go out of your way looking for them.

'A girl worthy of a future, Grim.'

'She isn't doing badly. She was on the cover of *Reveille* last week.'

'I mean the richer and fuller future that can come only to a happily married woman.'

'Oh, yes?'

'Let's face it, dear chappie – we did behave rather badly in her direction.'

'*We* did? Dash it! You were the one officially lined up to provide the richer and fuller future completely off your own bat.'

'There may have been some sort of informal arrangement.' Basil absently twisted a gold signet ring. 'But I'm thinking only of Ophelia's happiness. When you come down to it, I was nothing more than a mere strolling player. She would be far better off with a steady professional man like yourself.'

I said nothing.

'But don't you understand?' he insisted. 'I have given you Ophelia.'

'And I dashed well don't want her.'

Basil looked surprised. 'I thought you loved her?'

'She was merely another viper in my well-bitten bosom.'

'Oh, I see.'

He sat staring at the toes of his new shoes.

'A pity, because I was rather relying on you to get her out of my hair . . . I mean, to ensure her future happiness. Dear chappie, let me be perfectly frank. Our little Ophelia, as you know, is sometimes a rather headstrong girl.'

I nodded. 'Personally, I think she makes Salome look like Mrs Beeton.'

'And just before leaving the ship, when I dropped into her cabin to say good-bye, she did happen to mention . . . well, she said if I ever actually married Sybil van Barn, she'd come to the wedding and when they got to that awkward bit about knowing cause or just impediment why these two should not be joined together –'

'Stand up with a few well chosen words?'

'Exactly.' Basil nodded solemnly. 'It would be terribly damaging to my reputation on the stage. And to Sybil's feelings, of course. So I was wondering if you could possibly go round to have a word with the dear girl, and hand her this little present from Asprey's?'

He pulled out a blue leather case stuffed with diamonds.

'It would never do for Sybil to find I'd seen Ophelia myself, of course. In fact, she mustn't even know about this bracelet. Sybil's the most generous and understanding of women, but she does make me file a sort of expense sheet every month. I've put this down as fertilizer for the estate.'

I didn't know what to say. If I hadn't much wanted to see Basil after leaving the ship, I certainly never wanted to see Ophelia again at all. But as Basil and I had blown the whistle on our little feud I supposed I ought to help the idiot to give a smooth performance at his wedding, if only for the sake of the dear old digs.

'All right,' I agreed. 'I'll give her a ring tomorrow.'

'Dear chappie, that's absolutely splendid of you. How often have I said I could rely on Grimsdyke as a real true friend?' He glanced at his new wrist watch. 'I say, you'll have to get cracking with my examination. I'm due at an agency in Bond Street at four to interview some butlers. It's so terribly difficult to find the right type of English servant these days. I absolutely insist on paying for the treatment this time, of course. And by the way, dear chappie,' he added, as he started to unknot his new silk tie, 'on this occasion, perhaps you'd better send me the result of the laboratory test by post.'

19

'I gathered from Potter-Phipps in the St Swithin's private block yesterday that you have condescended to do a little medical work for a change,' said my cousin Miles.

'That's right,' I replied. 'Medicine is my legal spouse and literature my mistress. When I get tired of one I go and sleep with the other.'

'I suppose I should have expected you to make some stupid remark like that.'

'I didn't. It was Chekhov.'

Miles frowned. 'I do wish you'd grow out of this practice of scoring feeble points off me, Gaston. It was bad enough at school, when I recall you deliberately set out to undermine my authority as a prefect.'

I made no reply, while Miles drove his Alvis through the free-for-all round Hyde Park Corner. The trouble with my cousin, of course, was having no sense of humour. He still couldn't see the funny side of those cricket boots.

'I must really ask you to show some consideration for me,' Miles went on bitterly. 'Here am I, one of Her Majesty's Royal Commissioners, and you, my cousin, pursue a Bohemian existence in some squalid basement in Paddington.'

'Not out of choice, let me add,' I returned smartly. 'I'm not one for the crust of bread and your-tiny-hand-is-frozen stuff at all. If you'd only cough up some of that cash for me, I'd start wallowing in the shocking luxury of regular meals and a bit of fresh air.'

Miles tightened his lips. 'That is totally out of the question. You would merely squander it on some woman.'

'My dear old lad! I haven't seen the woman you mean for months, and I wouldn't much care if I never did again.'

'Indeed? I thought when we met a little earlier you had an appointment to visit her this evening?'

'Of course I did, dash it! But that was in quite a different connexion –'

'Please do not insult my intelligence with more of these feeble excuses.'

Miles swung his car round the policeman in Vauxhall Bridge Road, and pulled up sharply in the forecourt of Victoria Station.

I'd been having a difficult day of it. In the week since seeing Basil Beauchamp I'd had no luck ringing Ophelia's flat, but that morning I'd managed to catch her in her bath.

'Darling, I'm simply dripping,' she'd explained over the wire. 'But where on earth have you been? I haven't heard from you for ages and ages.'

'Overwork, you know. Terribly busy.'

'Yes, I'm utterly frantic, too.'

'I say, old girl,' I went on, coming briskly to business. 'How about a little drink together? Just for old time's sake.'

'But darling! I don't know when I'll ever have a spare evening again.'

'I've a rather important message for you,' I added urgently. 'Not to mention a jolly little present that will bring a sparkle to your life.'

'Oh, all right, darling.' She sounded doubtful. 'I think I can manage a quick one if you pick me up here at six.'

By doing without lunch I'd bought a bunch of flowers, and I was just leaving my basement when I noticed Miles' car crawling along the gutter.

'Gaston!' he called through the window. 'Do you realize I have been looking for you half over London? What conceivably made you hide yourself in this atrocious district?'

'Oh, hello, Miles. It's really quite attractive when the sun goes down over Wormwood Scrubs –'

'You are to accompany me to Sir Lancelot's house at once.'

'Sir Lancelot's house? But I'm afraid I've a rather pressing engagement –'

'You will simply have to put the lady off.' Miles glared at the flowers. 'Sir Lancelot particularly wishes you to come to dinner. We are informally entertaining the Home Secretary.'

'The Home Secretary?' I looked a bit blank. 'Good Lord! What on earth makes Sir Lancelot think he's anxious to get chummy with a chap like me?'

'Don't stand there making idiotic remarks. Please get in the car.'

'Oh, all right. I'll phone Ophelia and put her off. You can have the flowers for Bartholomew's nursery.'

I got the hang of my invitation as soon as we arrived at Sir Lancelot's house, when the surgeon opened the door himself in his shirt-sleeves and frilly apron.

'Delighted you're able to give us a hand in the crisis, my boy,' he greeted me. 'Can you cook?'

'As a matter of fact, sir, I do rather fancy my touch with an omelette,' I admitted.

'As a bachelor doing for himself you can presumably mix salad dressing? Then you will kindly accompany me to the kitchen and try. Miles, lay the table. And don't forget to polish the champagne glasses.'

'Haven't you got a maid yet, sir?' I asked, rather mystified as I followed Sir Lancelot through the house.

'It may interest you to know that the past two months of my life have been plagued by a succession of females, who have enjoyed in common a striking inability to master the rudiments of the English language and a morbidly hysterical personality. That is not to mention a lady from some obscure corner of the Alps, who arrived solely to have her infant at the expense of our over-solicitous Health Service. Fortunately, I have an eye for such things. All this has understandably tried the patience of both our excellent cook and myself. Our cook enjoyed the advantage of being able to pack up and leave.'

'Oh, I see, sir.'

I felt rather narked at being roped in for the evening as Sir Lancelot's skivvy instead of loading Ophelia with diamonds, but I remembered again that except for the old boy I'd have left St Swithin's before Christmas in one of the tasteful plain vans they keep for the purpose.

'My wife is at this very moment down at the agency, trying to discover where the devil our specially recommended mademoiselle from Paris has got to,' Sir Lancelot continued

'As the woman appears to be lost in transit and we can hardly put off a Cabinet minister, we have no alternative but to cook and bottle-wash ourselves.'

In the kitchen I found the Bishop, with his jacket off and black in the face.

'Confound it, Charles! Haven't you got the boiler working yet?'

'I fear, Lancelot, it is somewhat beyond me. It is really a most recalcitrant piece of apparatus. It seems quite to possess a personality of its own.'

'If you don't get the ruddy boiler going you'll have no hot water,' said Sir Lancelot shortly. 'And you know it's your turn to wash up.'

'I was just going to mention I have a rather nasty cut on my hand. I did it with the cucumber slicer. As you know, my flesh festers so easily, and I fear immersion in hot soapy water –'

'I don't give a damn whether you develop acute gas gangrene of the upper limb. It's still your turn to wash up.'

'You might show a little sympathy,' complained the Bishop.

'It was clearly understood weeks ago that whoever gets the early tea doesn't wash up. And this morning you chose to wallow in bed.'

'I tell you I woke with a most unpleasant headache –'

'So I had to boil your breakfast egg. *And* you pinched the ruddy *Times* –'

'I don't see why you can't order two copies of *The Times*,' returned the Bishop testily. 'You always make such a fuss about it.'

'So, you would lead me down the paths of gross extravagance?'

'There was something I particularly wanted to read about the Commission.'

'You didn't. You did the crossword. It was my morning for the crossword.'

'It wasn't your morning at all. You did the crossword yesterday.'

'Of course I did. You can hardly fail to remember you swapped an extra crossword for my cleaning the baths.'

'I am going to my room,' said the Bishop curtly. 'Apart from everything else, I have my headache again. Not to mention a considerable quantity of soot down my neck.'

'If that feller stays here any longer I'll sell the house to the demolition squad and take furnished lodgings.' Sir Lancelot handed me a salad bowl. 'You can't imagine how intolerable it is, with Maud pampering him at every turn. Only my natural good breeding prevents my dropping the hint that he has outstayed his welcome. The man has a hide like a – Ah, there you are, my dear. Any luck with the girl?'

'Everything's perfectly all right, Lancelot,' announced Lady Spratt breathlessly. 'Mademoiselle's boat was held up, that's all. She's due at Victoria in fifteen minutes.'

'Good,' exclaimed Sir Lancelot. 'Grimsdyke – *cherchez la femme.*'

'Me, sir?' I looked alarmed. 'But how would I recognize her, sir?'

'She'll be wearing lily of the valley and carrying a copy of *Paris Match*,' explained Lady Spratt quickly. 'Of course, she doesn't speak any English –'

'I'm not really much cop at the *défense d'afficher* stuff once I'm off a menu,' I told them doubtfully.

'Then for God's sake take someone with you,' directed Sir Lancelot impatiently. 'Take Miles. He once spent a fortnight at Dinard, and for months after seemed to imagine it made him an honorary member of the French Academy.'

As Miles had got into a frightful muddle with the fish forks, anyway, he was pleased enough to drive me to Victoria. Particularly as it gave a chance for one of those little lectures of his *en route*.

'It is really most unfortunate that Sir Lancelot cannot handle staff better,' he complained finally, as we got out of the car at the station. 'It will be highly distressing if the Home Secretary notices anything amiss. The Bishop and I are at pains to have him in the right frame of mind for discussing our minority views on the Commission.'

'How's the old immorality going?' I asked.

Miles looked pained. 'There is no need for you to be flippant, Gaston. You don't seem to realize what extremely arduous and distasteful work it is. I am obliged almost daily to observe things that surprise even me. Who could have imagined that all over London men sit for hours watching a succession of girls removing their clothing? Our modern civilization is gripped by a vast epidemic of voyeurism.'

I nodded. 'I remember the first case. It was reported in the year 1040, from Coventry –'

'You're an idiot,' said Miles, slamming the car door.

Personally, I've always found Victoria rather a jolly station. While other London termini lead nowhere more exciting than Glasgow, it's always a pretty sight on a winter's evening watching the happy-faced young holiday-makers tripping on to the departure platform with their skis on their shoulders, and hobbling off the arrival one with their plaster casts and crutches. And in summer there's the buckets and spades and bare knees and kiddies being sick in the booking office, and all the year round, come aeroplanes, come space rockets, I bet nobody fails to tingle a bit inside on spotting the sign CONTINENTAL DEPARTURES while running after a train for Balham.

'The boat train seems to be in already,' observed Miles, as we made our way through the crowd at the barrier.

'If you're feeling rocky on the lingo, the Man from Cook's over there is bursting to hold forth like Robespierre,' I mentioned.

'My dear Gaston, I do wish you would give me the credit for a little intelligence. We should anyway be able to identify the young woman perfectly easily. Lily of the valley is a fairly unusual flower.'

I nodded. 'She must be that grey-haired old dear over there with the hampers.'

Miles frowned.

'Or that kid sucking a stick of toffee. Or perhaps the bird with the moustache and the astrakhan collar? He's carrying a bunch of the stuff.' I gave a laugh. 'Do you know what day it is?'

'Day? May the first, of course.'

'Yes, the day the French buy it by the basketful and stick it all over themselves, except that they call it *muguet*.'

Miles bit his lip. 'How remarkably awkward.'

'Don't worry, there's still the magazine diagnosis.' I

searched the crowd. 'I say, how about that blonde over there?'

I began to feel I wouldn't mind doing Sir Lancelot's washing up after all.

'I doubt it. Lady Spratt explained she was a mature woman and most respectable, being the daughter of some minor *fonctionnaire*.'

My cousin looked on bleakly as a couple of nuns came through the barrier, followed by a file of schoolgirls covered with *muguet*. Then he started approaching unaccompanied females, raising his hat, and trying his '*Est-ce que vous êtes la bonne de* Sir Lancelot Spratt?' stuff, but this didn't get him more than a few dirty looks.

'You might do something to help,' he said impatiently, 'instead of just standing there putting pennies in the slot machines.'

'Bit peckish,' I explained. 'No lunch.'

'Blast you,' muttered Miles.

As a matter of fact, I was getting rather anxious as well, the platform now being empty except for some African chaps in robes, who obviously wouldn't have done at all. But just then a respectable looking middle-aged woman in a teddy-bear coat appeared round a pile of mail-bags, carrying a magazine and sprouting lily of the valley luxuriously.

'*Pardonnez-moi*,' Miles began again. '*Mais êtes-vous engagé à* Sir Lancelot Spratt?'

She gave a nice smile. '*Ce que vous êtes gentil*.'

'Thank God for that!' exclaimed Miles. 'Gaston, take the lady's case. *Par ici*, mademoiselle. *Nous avons l'auto dans* the *qu'est-ce que c'est* outside.'

'*Comment? Vous êtes venus me chercher en auto?*'

'*Seulement le meilleur est assez bon pour la bonne*,' I told her, feeling rather proud of myself on the spur of the moment.

We all three piled into the Alvis and bustled back to Harley Street.

20

'Morality is, after all, merely a matter of geographical latitude,' declared Sir Lancelot Spratt airily. 'What passes in polite society in Bali would never do in Berkeley Square.'

'Um, ah,' said the Bishop.

Miles had lit the boiler and cleaned him up a bit, and the four of us were taking a glass of sherry in the drawing-room while Lady Spratt installed the new maid upstairs.

'The unfortunate British public has been much exposed to moralists.' Sir Lancelot stood stroking his beard before the fireplace. 'Indeed, the population has hardly been allowed to pursue its natural instincts in peace since the arrival of Oliver Cromwell. No wonder our clinics are cluttered with the diseases of mass repression.'

Miles seemed to be fidgeting rather.

'I should have thought as a nation we were proud of our respectability, Lancelot.'

'And so we are, like our draughts and beastly trains and horrible climate and filthy cooking. At heart we are, of course, a shocking collection of masochists.'

'By the way, sir,' I intruded, 'now the domestic situation is under control, I expect you'd like me to clear off?'

Miles and the Bishop looked more cheerful at this, but Sir Lancelot replied:

'Certainly not. I invited you to dinner, and to dinner you stay. Not that I would deceive you our guest is a second Dr Johnson. Treating his varicose veins last year gave me an opportunity to break the ice, and I found myself paddling in some very cold water underneath.'

He helped us to more sherry.

'Grimsdyke and myself will anyway retire after dinner to discuss my memoirs,' he added to the others. 'How's the book coming along, my boy?'

'Almost finished, sir. I'm rather looking forward to rounding it all off with a jolly good trial scene, like *The Brothers Karamazov*.'

'Then you will be pleased to hear you haven't long to wait. In the confusion I quite overlooked telling you that Beckwith informs me the affair is down for hearing next Monday.'

'I can only hope, Lancelot, that truth will prevail,' observed the Bishop cagily.

'My dear good fellow, the facts of the case are perfectly indisputable. Even before a meddlesome crank like Mr Justice Fishwick –'

I looked up. 'Fishwick?'

'It is perhaps unfortunate that my trial should appear on his list. But Fishwick is nevertheless a member of an intelligent profession, like ourselves,' Sir Lancelot conceded, 'and I have no doubt whatever that he will find himself obliged to stop the proceedings before my brother has even been put to the trouble of opening his mouth.'

There was a ring at the doorbell.

'That can hardly be our distinguished guest so soon.' Sir Lancelot frowned at his watch. 'Grimsdyke, be a good fellow and answer it.'

On the step I found the police sergeant who'd brought the news from the Zoo, with a rather nice little blonde in a red coat.

'Good evening, sir.' He seemed very civil. 'I wonder if I might have a word with Sir Lancelot Spratt?'

I took another look at the girl, wondering whom she'd been feeding to the carnivores. Murmuring something about Sir Lancelot sparing a few moments, I led the sergeant into the drawing-room and left her in the hall.

'Why, it's Sergeant Griffin again.' Sir Lancelot greeted him warmly. 'How's the old rupture?'

'Very nicely, thank you, sir.'

'I'm delighted to hear it. Glass of sherry?'

'No, thank you, Sir Lancelot.'

'I believe you've met the Bishop of Wincanton?'

His brother-in-law was at the time trying to dodge behind the azalea.

'You've come about the security arrangements, I suppose, officer?' suggested Miles.

The sergeant raised his eyebrows. 'Security arrangements, sir?'

Miles looked faintly uneasy.

'Perhaps,' he added hopefully, 'it's simply that my car is causing an obstruction outside?'

'No, it's about your girl, sir.'

'My girl?' asked Sir Lancelot.

'The young lady you was to meet off the train from Paris.'

'I hope she is in every way quite respectable,' interrupted the Bishop quickly.

'She seems a very respectable young person indeed, sir. She was lost, that's all. The Railway Police sent her from Victoria, and I've brought her round.'

'But that's absolutely ridiculous!' Miles gave a laugh. 'Because the girl in question is already in –'

'Quite, Sergeant, quite,' Sir Lancelot broke in. 'Thank you very much. The young lady is outside? Excellent. We were wondering what had happened to her. Sorry you've been put to such trouble.'

'Nothing's too much trouble for you, Sir Lancelot. As a matter of fact, I was rather wanting to have a word about my operation –'

'Another time, Sergeant, another time.'

'It's only that I have a sort of tickling feeling in the scar.' The policeman seemed inclined for a chat. 'I was wondering if you could take a quick look at it for me?'

'Call tomorrow and I shall be delighted.'

'It's more of a cross between a tickling and an itching sensation –'

'So this is the young lady?' Sir Lancelot hustled him through the door. '*Enchanté, mademoiselle.* My dear,' he added, as Lady Spratt appeared on the stairs. 'Here is our new maid from Paris. Kindly show her to the second spare room.'

'Lancelot, have you completely taken leave of your –'

'This is the *new maid,*' repeated Sir Lancelot forcefully. 'Upstairs, please, *s'il vous plaît,* pronto.'

'Look here –' started Miles, looking as confused as the girl while she was led away. 'I don't at all understand –'

'I most sincerely trust nothing untoward –' murmured the Bishop.

'You want to be on your way, no doubt, Sergeant,' Sir Lancelot interrupted both of them. 'It was extremely helpful of you to call.'

'I was wondering, sir, if you would do us the honour of attending our next social evening?'

'I should be delighted. I expect you are now extremely busy –'

'Old tyme dancing, you know. With a buffet and extension till midnight.'

'It sounds extremely charming. I shall certainly attend.'

'As it happens, I've a book of tickets on me.'

'I'll take the lot.' Sir Lancelot edged him on to the front step. 'My cheque will reach you in the morning.'

'But there's over a hundred tickets there, Sir Lancelot!'

'I have a very large number of friends,' Sir Lancelot pushed him through the door. 'Now gentlemen –' He faced the three of us. 'The question is – Who the devil have we already installed upstairs?'

'But she *must* be your maid.' Miles looked annoyed. 'She certainly said she was. Besides, she was carrying that magazine on the table.'

'Which happens to be *L'Illustration*.'

'So it is,' said Miles in surprise.

'It is highly unfortunate we should be involved in any complications,' muttered the Bishop.

'I'm sure it can be perfectly easily cleared up,' Miles protested. 'She was certainly a most decent person. Wasn't she, Gaston?'

'Well, you'd better go and break it to her that she's due for a change of address,' Sir Lancelot told him.

'But where to?' I interrupted.

'That is for your cousin Miles to find out.'

'I think you're all making far too much of a perfectly excusable mistake,' returned Miles shortly.

Sir Lancelot became impatient.

'We can settle all that at our leisure. Instead of standing

there wasting time, go upstairs and find out exactly where the poor woman belongs.'

Miles hesitated.

'Perhaps Gaston would like to ask her –'

'No I jolly well wouldn't! Anyway, you told me you were the expert on French.'

'It might be politic to clear up the little matter at once,' urged the Bishop.

'Damn it, Miles!' exploded Sir Lancelot. 'You can at least try and find out what she does for a living.'

But this turned out to be unnecessary, because Miles had hardly got a foot on the stairs before the girl appeared herself.

'Horror!' exclaimed the Bishop.

A bit of a change had come over our middle-aged dear from Victoria Station. In the first place, she was made up as brightly as the lights of Piccadilly. In the second, she'd got on a red wig about a foot high. In the third, she was wearing only a large pink fan.

'Good gracious me,' remarked Sir Lancelot Spratt.

She gave a nice smile from the landing.

''Ullo, boys. We start the show, yes?'

'But – but this is impossible!' cried Miles.

''Ow nice I find your English clubs.' She undulated downstairs. 'So correct. *Très anglais.*' She patted the Bishop on the cheek. 'I am shocking, eh?'

'Horror upon horror,' muttered the Bishop.

'Miles!' Sir Lancelot gave a roar of laughter. 'You know what you are? A blasted *procureur*.'

I hadn't seen the poor chap in such a state since the headmaster found he was keeping white mice in the dormitory.

'Do something!' he burst out. 'Do something at once! Lancelot – Gaston – you must get that woman away from here –'

'You found her,' Sir Lancelot told him briefly. 'You lose her again.'

'Gaston!' Miles grabbed my arm. 'You're my cousin . . . you must help, you understand? I implore you. My whole career –'

The girl winked at Sir Lancelot. 'You want to come an' see me after the show?'

'The extreme kindness of your invitation, madam, quite shames my inescapable refusal.'

She picked the Bishop's official topper from the hat-stand, and put it on like Marlene Dietrich in *The Blue Angel*.

'I feel faint,' cried the Bishop, falling into a chair.

'A family weakness, Charles.' Sir Lancelot seemed to be enjoying himself like young Bartholomew on Christmas morning. 'You know where to find the brandy.'

'My God!' gasped Miles. 'If this got in the papers –'

'Papers!' The Bishop fluttered his handkerchief. 'I must leave. I must leave at once –'

'Yes, I think the country would be much kinder to your constitution,' Sir Lancelot agreed calmly. 'I shall call you personally at six –'

The girl threw aside her fan, and stood wearing only the Bishop's hat like a sort of muff.

'What on earth's the matter with you, Charles?' demanded Sir Lancelot. 'Really! It's only a healthy naked human female.'

'I shall leave this very night –'

'There is an excellent late train. And my car is always at your disposal for the station.'

The girl started to get a bit playful with the hat.

'I'm going to be sick,' announced the Bishop.

'But surely, Charles, you are not going to miss your dinner?'

'Dinner!' Miles jumped. 'He'll be arriving in twenty minutes!'

'Look here –' I was becoming rather worried myself. 'We'd really better do something, and pretty smartly.'

My cousin and I may have suffered our little disagreements in the past, but I felt that bringing them up now would be like complaining the bedclothes were damp because the ship was sinking. Personally, I'm rather fond of a bit of cabaret with my dinner, but I could see that under present circumstances it would never have done for old Miles at all. As the Bishop was looking as though he'd come off the operating table after a total gastrectomy, Sir Lancelot was stroking his beard in perplexity, and Miles seemed on the point of hysteria, I thought it was time to take sole charge.

'It's perfectly simple,' I suggested. 'The girl's probably been booked for a show at some Soho club. All we've got to do is get her there, and look jolly quick about it. Apart from anything else, I expect they're playing the overture over and over again waiting for her.'

'Where do you think you are, *madame*?' Miles burst out. '*Où croyez-vous que vous êtes?*'

She looked surprised behind the hat. '*Mais c'est* Willie's Club, *n'est-ce pas*?'

'Willie's Club!' muttered Miles.

'Dear old Willie's Club?' I exclaimed. 'But I'm a member. Willie and I were great pals in the days when I was one of the lads at St Swithin's. You go downstairs in Frith Street and there's a barman who's done Lord knows how many years in –'

'But damn it, Gaston!' exploded Miles. 'You can't appear with a half-naked woman like that! It would be bound to leak out to the press.'

'You've a good bit to learn about immorality yet, old lad,' I grinned. 'How much lolly have you got on you?'

'Money? About twenty pounds.'

'Let's have a bit of a whip-round then. May I borrow your Rolls, sir?'

'I shall accompany you,' said Sir Lancelot at once. 'Thank heavens somebody in your family has a little sense. Miles, fetch my Ulster for the lady. You will kindly tell our distinguished guest that I have been called to an urgent case. It is fortunate that our profession always provides a foolproof excuse. Come, *madame*. Let us now retrace our *faux pas*.'

'I am going to die,' groaned the Bishop.

'Really, Charles, that is most inconsiderate of you. Just think of the trouble all of us have taken over your dinner.'

21

'Miles hasn't been to the hospital today,' announced his wife Connie when I called at their house the following evening. 'The poor dear isn't at all himself. It's the strain of overwork on the Commission.'

I felt slightly put out, having planned to make myself comfortable and drink his whisky and soda until he arrived. Instead, I found my cousin in his shirt-sleeves pacing up and down among his Morality papers, looking like a prophet of doom in search of a pulpit.

'Hello, old lad,' I greeted him. 'How did the little dinner go?'

Miles groaned.

'It was like some horrible, horrible hallucination . . . That dreadful woman!'

'Clementine turned out to be quite a jolly sort in the end. We got to know her pretty well by the time we'd carted her across London.'

'What happened?' he asked gloomily.

'Everything went as smoothly as one of Sir Lancelot's appendicectomies. Even though I hadn't been in Willie's for years, at least I knew the drill for all irregularities on the premises, from trying to tickle the hostesses to trying to flog a machine-gun.'

'Bribery?' murmured Miles dully.

'Cash certainly changed hands. Ruddy great wads of it, in fact, from Sir Lancelot's wallet.'

My cousin fell silent.

'You might at least have returned and told us things were straightened out,' he said at last. 'The suspense was perfectly terrible.'

'It was Sir Lancelot's fault. He insisted on seeing the show.'

'He must have thought it thoroughly disgusting.'

'He seemed to find it rather amusing. Not to mention diagnosing a genu varum, two epigastric hernias, and several cases of diffuse mammary hypertrophy.'

'Sir Lancelot is perfectly incorrigible.'

'He helped save your bacon, old lad,' I reminded him. 'The whole country might have enjoyed the smell of it frying for breakfast this morning.'

He looked up. 'I suppose there *is* nothing in the press?'

I shook my head. 'I've been through every paper in the public library. Though, of course, there's always Sunday and the *News of the World*.'

Miles groaned again.

'But don't worry, I'm sure there's no harm done. Clementine got a terrific reception from the customers at Willie's, by the way. Though personally I think she was rather better with the hat.'

'I am, of course, enormously indebted to you, Gaston,' Miles admitted.

'Don't mention it,' I returned lightly. 'After all, same flesh and blood, and all that.'

'My whole career now lies at the mercy of your discretion.'

'Good Lord, you don't suppose I'd sneak, do you?' I looked shocked. 'Dash it, I didn't even do that at school when you pinched my special seed-cake.'

'I am sorry about the seed-cake, Gaston. Deeply sorry.'

'I'm quite prepared to forget it,' I told him, very decently.

'Would you care for a whisky and soda? Do help yourself. Take as much as you like.' As I accepted the invitation, he went on, 'We have admittedly had our differences in the past –'

'Clash of temperaments. Very stimulating to any family. Look at the Lears.'

Miles fiddled with a page of his Report.

'I must confess, Gaston, that over the years I have automatically come to look upon you as a fool.'

'The gay exterior is deceiving.'

'But the way you took charge of an extremely dangerous and complicated situation last night suddenly opened my eyes to your true abilities.'

'Oh, come! Once faced with the bare facts –' I gave a laugh. 'Rather funny, that.'

'How often have I secretly envied your sense of humour!'

'Tut, now,' I consoled the chap. 'You used to tell some jolly funny jokes yourself at the school concert.'

'You have the stuff in you of the Scarlet Pimpernel, Gaston. You are no mere theorist like myself and – may I say? – my colleagues on the Royal Commission. No. You are a man of action. At last I see it. And it has helped me to make my decision about the funds I hold in trust for you.'

'Funny, I was just coming to that,' I told him, preparing to put the screws on. 'If you'll just give me the cheque, I won't keep you any longer from your work.'

Miles stroked his little bristly moustache.

'When you first started this novel writing business I rather objected. I felt that the notoriously lax life of an author would be completely demoralizing for you.'

'Quite.'

It is, of course, well known to the British public that authors lounge about all day with their collars off while everyone else has to work.

'To be frank, I was not particularly concerned over your loss to medicine.'

'I think that's a matter of general agreement.'

'But now I have changed my mind.'

'If you'll just write out that cheque –'

'Don't you realize? Don't you see?' Miles gripped my sleeve. 'In this modern age you are exactly the sort of man our profession needs.'

'That didn't seem the view of all those examiners I got quite chummy with over the years.'

'But that's precisely the point, Gaston. What's wrong with medicine today?'

'Not enough pay –'

'We are all far too theoretical. We need practical men. Men like yourself. Men to penetrate the undeveloped ends of the earth, and blaze a trail of sanitation.'

'Here, hold on!' I exclaimed, a bit alarmed. 'I wouldn't be any use at that sort of lark at all. You know how I come up all over from mosquitoes.'

'Fortunately there are no mosquitoes in the area I have in mind. An international health team is shortly starting work on the shores of Greenland –'

'Greenland? Now look here, Miles, stop horsing about and make out that cheque –'

'I propose to finance you for a six months' refresher course in New York, after which I can easily arrange through my connexions with World Health Organization your appointment to a five years' tour in Greenland.'

'If you simply want to get me out of the way for a bit,' I interrupted, 'it would be much easier to slip me the cash and let me clear off to Paris.'

'I assure you that's not the idea at all.'

'Last time you shoved me up the ruddy Amazon. This time you want to keep me on ice. I wish you'd make up your mind.'

'But Gaston! Don't you realize what I am offering you? The chance to become a second Dr Livingstone. A Schweitzer of the snows.'

'Just let me have the cash on the nail. Apart from anything else, the rent for my basement is shockingly overdue.'

Miles looked pained. 'Surely you are not contemplating refusal?'

'Yes, I jolly well am. I've got a novel to finish.'

'But damnation! You don't seriously intend to fritter away your life turning out stupid books –'

'My dear good idiot! Once you start you can't stop – it's a sort of ineradicable infection. Anyway,' I added, now pretty narked, 'if somebody's got to go charging down glaciers with a syringe, why not you? You'd be a ruddy sight more use than sitting in London trying to explain why people shouldn't play football on Sundays.'

'I don't think you are being particularly grateful, Gaston.'

'Let's cut out all the fuss and simply hand over the cheque –'

Miles folded his arms. 'That is out of the question.'

'I like that! Who's being grateful now?'

'I have made an extremely generous offer.'

'It would be, if I were a homesick Eskimo.'

'Consider how much you could enjoy yourself in New York first.'

'Yes, thinking gaily of the future among all those ice cubes.'

'Don't you understand? Professionally speaking, I am trying to save your soul – What are you doing with that telephone?'

'Ringing up every number in Fleet Street to let a particularly nasty-looking cat out of the bag.'

'You wouldn't,' said Miles quietly.

I paused.

Of course, the chap had me there. Miles may have been a fool. He may have cheerfully left me to starve in basements. He may have given me a rotten time over those cricket boots. He may even have pinched my last bit of seed-cake. But there are certain things a chap doesn't do.

I replaced the receiver.

'You accept my offer?' asked Miles.

'No.'

He sighed. 'I must say I am sincerely sorry. You are leaving so soon?'

I didn't even finish my whisky.

22

'The honorarium for my memoirs? By all means, my dear fellow,' said Sir Lancelot. 'I shall put the cheque in the post tomorrow. You will understand that I am a little too preoccupied to attend to it this very morning.'

'Oh, quite, sir. Forgive my mentioning it at all.'

'I am sorry you are feeling the pinch of poverty, Grimsdyke. I always assumed from Miles that you had liquid assets.'

'A bit of a freeze seems to have set in at the moment,' I explained.

I'd had a pretty miserable few days in the basement. Razzy had a row with his opera singer you could hear all the way from Covent Garden to Charing Cross, so he could last through his afternoons again. My landlady was indicating that I'd shortly be taking up residence in the street. Worse still, the weather stayed absolutely beastly all the week-end. 'A duller spectacle this earth of ours has not to show than a rainy Sunday in London,' said De Quincey, and look what happened to him.

But I still had my duty towards Sir Lancelot, and on Monday morning interrupted my scheduled activities on the novel to appear at his house with a new notebook and accompany him to court. I still had my duty towards old Basil, too, I remembered, as we drove past Ophelia twelve feet high explaining how she liked a nice milky night-time drink.

'Darling,' she'd said, when I'd telephoned again a couple of days before and caught her doing the washing. 'It's absolutely impossible to spare a minute. I'm just dashing out again this evening.'

'It's a rather important message, old girl,' I returned solemnly. 'From Basil.'

'Basil? Basil who?'

'Basil Beauchamp.'

'You can tell that stage-struck oaf that if he thinks he can go round haunting me like some pantomime demon –'

'Quite the opposite, I assure you. He wants me to hand you a rather nice little parting present. It glitters.'

There was hesitation on the wire.

'Oh, all right, darling. Give me a ring tomorrow. I might be able to fit you in.'

But as usual she wasn't at home, and it took a good deal of the Grimsdyke strength of character to avoid using the bracelet as a chaser for the grandpa's cuff-links.

'What do you think of our chances, Grimsdyke?' Sir Lancelot interrupted my thoughts in the traffic that raced round Trafalgar Square, now enjoying a bright May morning's sunshine.

'I should think, sir, that a high-powered barrister like your brother ought to impress the beak –'

'Good gracious, I mean in the Test Matches. The other matter is perfectly open and shut. You know, of course, who is giving evidence as the expert witness against me?'

'Lord Tiptree, I thought, sir?'

Sir Lancelot turned his Rolls into the Strand.

'I must apologize for not informing you before that Clem Tiptree was unexpectedly called to lecture in Australia. His place has been taken by that nasty little man McFiggie.'

'McFiggie, sir?'

'But as the feller has to my certain knowledge never stuck a knife into living flesh for his entire professional career, I cannot understand anyone being interested for a minute in his views on clinical surgery. Or on anything else much, for that matter.'

'He's got a terrific reputation in the courts,' I mentioned cagily.

'Clem Tiptree was prepared to stand up and attack me in public because he was handsomely paid for it,' Sir Lancelot went on, ignoring this. 'And I don't blame him. But McFiggie is unhappily motivated by personal spite. He has become remarkably unfriendly since I was obliged to put him in his place over spreading scurrilous stories about me round the hospital. But here we are at the Law Courts, Grimsdyke. Now the fun begins.'

The old boy seemed in a cracking mood. I supposed it was because he'd had *The Times* to himself that morning, not to mention wallowing in the Bishop's share of the bathwater.

I'd never been in the Royal Courts of Justice before, my own little brushes with the Law being settled in those depressing rooms round the back of town halls. The place struck me as needing a few slot machines and a bit of steam to turn it into a jolly good railway station. It was filled with severe looking birds in wigs hurrying past at a tremendous rate, I suppose like the doctors at St Swithin's, to give onlookers the impression that chaps of their importance were wanted pretty damn urgently somewhere. One or two seedy-looking coves wandered about with armfuls of equally decayed reference books, a couple of old dears were mopping the floor, and the only representative of legal majesty was a porter in a little round cap like a Victorian warder, sitting by the door reading the *Daily Mirror*.

'*Possett v. Spratt*, Court Sixteen,' read Sir Lancelot from the notices displayed like train timetables in the middle of the hall.

He clasped his hands under the tails of his coat. The old boy had appeared in full morning dress and cravat, which I supposed he felt the correct costume for being sued.

'I only wish we had time to hear some of the other cases,' he remarked. 'What, for instance, could Imperial Crab Fisheries possibly be suing Swindon Hosiery manufacturers about? Or Ebineezer Novelties the Home for Indigent Gentlewomen? Perfectly intriguing! But we must not delay, Grimsdyke. Beckwith is meeting us at the Court.'

Mr Beckwith now had the brightly confident air of a family doctor shepherding his patient into hospital for a major operation.

'What's happened to Alfie?' demanded Sir Lancelot at once.

Mr Beckwith explained the Q.C. was several corridors

away, urging the complaint of a poultry breeder against an incinerator manufacturer.

'An absolute disgrace,' Sir Lancelot snorted. 'What do you imagine they'd say at St Swithin's if I left in the middle of a pancreatectomy to remove a pair of tonsils? The administration of justice in this country is laughably haphazard. Which I suppose is all you can expect when everyone gives themselves thumping long holidays and knocks off at four.'

'I'm afraid there's a slight delay with your case, anyway,' Mr Beckwith apologized. 'Apparently Fishwick is rather bilious this morning, and wants a short rest.'

'Damnation! If I held up my entire theatre staff every time I felt a bit off-colour –'

'Fishwick always takes very good care of himself, Sir Lancelot.'

'Another way of saying the feller's a shocking hypochondriac, as I could have told you years ago. I wonder what the devil he did with my fountain-pen in the end, anyway?'

We filed into the court, which was all carved oak canopies, ink-stained forms and varnish, and struck me as a cross between a revivalist chapel and the lecture room at St Swithin's.

There were more seedy-looking chaps messing about with books, and an usher in a gown who seemed to be asleep, and we all three sat on a bench while Mr Beckwith started going through his bundles of papers. After about half an hour the room started to fill up, there was a bit of muttering all round, the usher woke up and opened a door behind the bench, and everyone stood up politely as Mr Justice Fishwick appeared.

I was pretty interested to take a look at Sir Lancelot's former fellow lodger, who was a long thin chap with a long thin nose and long thin earpieces on his gold-rimmed glasses. There was a good deal of fussing as a tartan rug was tucked round his knees and a couple of bottles of white pills placed next to the judicial water-jug, then he stared round as though wondering how we'd all been let in from the street, and the case of Possett *v.* Spratt began.

'My Lord –'

A fat, red-faced barrister like a bewigged bookie stood up. Now I come to think of it, all English judges are pretty thin and all English barristers are pretty portly, I suppose through all those dinners they make them eat.

'My Lord,' said the barrister, after explaining who he was and which side he was on. 'I can put my case very briefly –'

'I am glad to hear it, Mr Grumley. The longer we are here, the longer we are dissipating public money.'

'Quite so, My Lord. I am very much indebted for Your Lordship's most salutary reminder.'

'Please get on, Mr Grumley.'

'He's in a pretty bad mood this morning,' whispered Mr Beckwith, seeming to be familiar with the signs and symptoms.

'The feller always had a nasty little temper,' agreed Sir Lancelot under his breath. 'Particularly when he'd eaten something that made him itch a bit.'

'I well know Your Lordship's concern over expedition of the Court's business,' continued the fat barrister fruitily. 'I much appreciate Your Lordship's consideration in drawing attention so early –'

'Get on with your case, get on with your case,' muttered the Judge.

'As Your Lordship pleases. I was saying, My Lord –'

'You haven't said anything yet, Mr Grumley.'

'Hasn't changed a bit,' hissed Sir Lancelot, slapping his thigh.

Mr Grumley finally hit form, and delivered a speech with the general effect of making Sir Lancelot Spratt look like Sweeney Todd the Barber. The surgeon meanwhile sat beside me staring at his finger-nails, giving no hint of his feelings apart from turning steadily from pink to magenta.

'I now call my first witness,' he ended. 'Herbert Egbert Thomas Possett.'

'Herbert Egbert Thomas Possett,' repeated the usher, waking up.

Sir Lancelot's patient was a vacant-looking youth in a tight blue suit, with the air of wishing he were at that moment in the middle of the Sahara desert. He started off by giving his name, address, birthday and date of admission to St Swithin's Hospital, none of which he seemed particularly sure about.

'Now, Mr Possett.' Mr Grumley came to business. 'What exactly was your operation performed for?'

There was a silence, except for the judge tapping his false teeth with his pencil.

'I dunno.'

'What? Didn't the surgeon tell you?'

'Nobody told me nothing.'

Mr Justice Fishwick cleared his throat.

'I have stated before in this Court, and I have no hesitation in stating it again, that the manner in which the medical profession keeps its patients in utter ignorance of matters of life and death is perfectly reprehensible. It is nothing more than an ill-judged attempt to perpetuate the aura of obscurity and witchcraft in which doctors have delighted in wrapping themselves for generations.'

'What absolute rubbish!' exclaimed Sir Lancelot.

'Shhhh!' hissed his brother, who had mysteriously appeared among us.

'Why, hello, Alfie! I was just beginning to wonder where the devil you'd got to. Fishwick has just made a perfectly outrageous remark –'

'Be quiet, please,' muttered Mr Beckwith.

'But it *is* outrageous,' persisted the surgeon.

'Silence!' cried the usher, whom I thought was fast asleep.

'Mr Spratt.' The Judge scowled at the Q.C. and then at Sir Lancelot. 'Perhaps you can kindly control your client?'

'I am extremely sorry, My Lord. I apologize most freely to Your Lordship. I fear my client suffered a momentary lapse.'

'I trust he will not suffer anything worse. Please proceed, Mr Grumley.'

Sir Lancelot glared at his brother in disgust. 'Despicable boot licking,' he muttered.

I was rather relieved myself when everything settled down for a bit. Young Prossett recited a list of symptoms he'd suffered since his operation, which ranged from going to sleep over the telly to fits. Mr Grumley, the crafty chap, kept asking if he wanted to sit, have a glass of water, or take a nice lie down for half an hour, and generally gave the impression that he, for one, was enormously surprised to see the poor fellow walking about at all.

'I have no question, My Lord,' announced Alfie, as his rival finished.

'Call Mrs Possett,' said Mr Grumley.

23

Herbert's mother was one of those little sharp-faced women you often see waving umbrellas at motorists from the middle of zebra crossings.

'It's a crying shame,' she began at once.

'Quite,' said Mr Grumley.

'A perfect disgrace.'

'Quite. Now, when your son was admitted to St Swithin's Hospital –'

'He was a fine healthy boy. And look at him now. Just look at him! Can hardly eat his dinner, he can't. Not without pangs. Pangs, that's what he has.'

'Yes, quite, Mrs Possett.' Mr Grumley began to look as though he wished he were in the middle of the Sahara, too. 'When your son was admitted –'

'I know. I'm a mother. I know.'

'I am sure we all, His Lordship included – particularly His Lordship – sympathize with a mother's distress. But if you will kindly tell the Court when your son was –'

'Indigestion?' the Judge asked her bleakly.

'Something cruel, Your Lordship.'

'I have suffered from it all my life. I fear it is hopelessly beyond the ability of the medical profession to cure. Please proceed, Mr Grumley.'

'Did you hear that, Alfie?' demanded Sir Lancelot loudly.

'Shut up, Lancelot.'

The surgeon looked shocked. 'What the devil do you mean, "Shut up"? I am trying to assist you by pointing out a blatant piece of misinformation –'

'Silence!' shouted the usher, and went to sleep again like Alice's dormouse.

'Proceed, Mr Grumley.' The Judge gave a stare in our

direction that looked as unfriendly as a trephine. Sir Lancelot sat muttering, but the only words I could distinguish were 'Star Chamber'.

We had peace for half an hour, while Mrs Possett described how Sir Lancelot had turned her son from something like Tarzan into the present dyspeptic wreck.

'To what, Mrs Possett,' demanded Mr Alphonso Spratt, rising on his brother's behalf, 'do you ascribe your son's present indisposition?'

'To 'im down there!' She pointed at Sir Lancelot like a *sans-culotte* having a go at the aristocrats. ''E's the one what's gone and ruined our Herbert. I don't care what nobody says about –'

'Madam!' Sir Lancelot leapt to his feet. 'It is quite bad enough for a man in my position to be dragged into a public court at all, but to be subject to ill-mannered harangues –'

'Sit down,' snapped the Judge.

'Really, Your Lordship! If you cannot in your own court control the irresponsible accusations –'

'Sit down!'

Mr Beckwith and I pulled Sir Lancelot to his seat.

'Silence!' cried the usher, having woken up a bit late.

'Mr Spratt –' said the Judge.

'May I assure you, My Lord, I do most humbly –'

'Mr Spratt, after your cross-examination you will kindly enlighten your client on the penalties for contempt of court.'

'Yes, My Lord. Of course, of course, My Lord. I am very grateful to My Lord –'

'I would advise you to be perfectly explicit.'

'Naturally, My Lord. I am much indebted to Your Lordship's most thoughtful suggestion.' He turned to glare at his brother. 'You bloody fool,' he hissed.

'Proceed,' added the Judge.

Sir Lancelot sat breathing heavily. I edged up a bit and sat on one of his coat tails.

'Dr Angus McFiggie,' announced Mr Grumley, when Mrs Possett had escaped.

The Judge looked up.

'Your only expert, Mr Grumley?'

'He is, My Lord.'

'I am quite prepared to hear his evidence, but from what has passed already I feel it my duty to suggest to the defendant, in the interests of saving my time and public money, that he should seriously consider the possibility of a settlement. I am perfectly willing to grant an adjournment for the purpose.'

Sir Lancelot looked as if a junior nurse at St Swithin's had contradicted his diagnosis.

'What a preposterous suggestion!'

'Will you be quiet, Lancelot?' snapped his brother.

'I wish you'd make up your mind, Alfie,' returned the surgeon angrily, 'exactly which side you are on.'

'I take it you are disinclined to settle?' demanded Mr Justice Fishwick bleakly.

'Never!' Sir Lancelot folded his arms.

'I will charitably assume the defendant's refusal to be uttered by counsel, who is the only person entitled to address the Court. You will explain that to him as well, Mr Spratt.'

'I am most indebted for Your Lordship's most helpful and considerate –'

'Proceed, Mr Grumley.'

As McFiggie appeared in the box Beckwith passed me a note saying, 'Hope Sir Lancelot is a sporting loser.' I thought it best to make no reply.

I must say, I felt pretty miserable about the morning's proceedings. Apart from Sir Lancelot's saving the Grimsdyke life, I'd developed a pretty strong respect for the old boy in our adventures over the last few months. It was pretty galling to see him not only going down the legal drain, but being treated by Fishwick much the same as I was treated myself by Miles.

McFiggie was, of course, totally different from the chap who'd sat sucking his teeth in Sir Lancelot's drawing-room. He was as at home in the Court as in the saloon bar of his local. He stood glaring round, his eyebrows slowly going up and down like a pair of peculiar hairy insects likely to fly off and sting someone. Even Mr Justice Fishwick seemed impressed, and helped himself to a couple of pills and a glass of water.

'Dr McFiggie,' began Mr Grumley, after reciting our pathologist's qualifications and appointments like reading out a Royal Proclamation. 'Would you say, on the basis of your many – your many and most highly valued – years as a specialist in forensic medicine, that the symptoms complained of by Mr Possett are a perfectly possible result of his operation?'

'I would.'

Sir Lancelot growled.

'You mean to tell the Court that the present pitiful condition of this previously healthy and virile young man might indeed have resulted from the operative interference of the defendant?'

'It might.'

I anchored Sir Lancelot a bit more firmly.

'Dr McFiggie, have you performed post-mortem examinations on the defendant's deceased patients?'

'I have.'

'And is it your opinion that in many cases the operation performed was necessary or unnecessary?'

'Unnecessary.'

Sir Lancelot jumped up, ripping off a coat-tail.

'I challenge that!'

'Silence!' called several people at once.

'I challenge McFiggie to produce one jot of clinical evidence –'

'Sit down and shut up!' snapped his brother.

'You keep out of this, Alfie –'

There was a good deal of confusion, through which I could hear the Judge shouting at someone to send for the Tipstaff.

'It is perfectly clear to the meanest intelligence you have not the slightest idea what you're talking about, McFiggie,' Sir Lancelot persisted hotly. 'If you had taken the bother to look up an elementary students' surgical textbook –'

'Sir Lancelot Spratt!' The Judge turned pale. 'I intend to commit you to Brixton Prison.'

Sir Lancelot stared at him. 'You intend to *what*?'

'I intend to commit you for contempt.'

'Oh, God,' muttered Mr Beckwith.

I didn't know what to say. I could only see our distinguished consultant – the chap who'd slammed death's door in my face – shuffling about in broad arrows breaking stones.

'Alfie, put this matter straight at once,' Sir Lancelot commanded.

'Damnation, Lancelot! If you insist on behaving without the least vestige of respect –'

'Mr Spratt!' rapped out the Judge.

'I am sorry, My Lord. Extremely sorry. I beg Your Lordship's pardon. I can only say –'

'If you'd controlled your client properly this unhappy situation would never have arisen.'

'Control him? You try and control him –'

'Mr Spratt!'

'I'm sorry, My Lord. Extremely sorry. This case has left me quite overwrought.'

'Look here, Alfie, I am perfectly certain a judge in a civil action hasn't the slightest right to make threats like that.'

'For God's sake, Lancelot! Can't you shut your big mouth?'

'Mr Spratt! Your language!'

'Dammit! Fishy, don't you see I'm at the end of my blasted tether?' complained Alfie. 'I warned you in the club last night my brother's completely impossible. I mean, I crave Your Lordship's pardon –'

'Stop crawling, Alfie,' urged Sir Lancelot. 'It makes me want to vomit.'

'Control your client, I say!'

'I'm doing my level best,' exclaimed Alfie angrily. 'But you're not making it any easier sitting up there threatening to hand out terms of imprisonment –'

'Mr Spratt! You forget yourself –'

'As a matter of fact, it's about time somebody protested from the Bar about the way you've been carrying on recently towards a perfectly respectable succession of litigants –'

'That's the stuff, Alfie!'

The Judge jumped up. 'I intend to commit you *both* to Brixton Prison.'

'What?' Alfie stopped short. 'But that's absolutely –'

'Where's the Tipstaff? Summon the Tipstaff! Send for the –'

I was just wondering whether to cause a diversion by setting a match to the papers, when the Judge gave a groan, reached for his pill bottle, and pitched over his desk.

'Good gracious me,' exclaimed Sir Lancelot. 'Grimsdyke!'

'Sir?'

'Hand me that water bottle. Right you are, everyone. I'll take charge. McFiggie – don't just stand there, pick up his feet. I recall now he did this once before, when I brought a foot home from the anatomy rooms for a lark and put it in his bed.'

24

Sir Lancelot and I sat alone in his drawing-room.

He'd only bothered to switch on one light, which gave an even gloomier air to the evening. We were sipping a whisky and soda in silence. Lady Spratt was up in Hampstead trying to engage another domestic. The new French maid had already left.

'Today,' observed Sir Lancelot at last. 'Is my birthday.'

There was another silence.

'Many . . . many happy returns, sir.'

'Thank you, Grimsdyke.'

We said nothing for a further five minutes.

'I suppose I was rather impetuous in court this morning,' Sir Lancelot admitted.

'Very understandable, sir,' I murmured.

'On the contrary, it was very stupid of me. Unfortunately, that is the nature of the beast.'

'A very useful quality, sometimes, sir,' I tried to console him.

'I suppose I can say that I have saved a life or two in my time by rushing in where angels and my fellow-surgeons have feared to tread,' he agreed quietly.

He sat for a few moments stroking his beard.

'There is a penalty to pay for being temporarily the most important person in the lives of our several patients,' he went on. 'If one is treated like a god day in and day out, it requires greater strength of character than I fear I possess not to feel oneself somewhat godlike. Indeed, one deliberately plays the part – call it a bedside manner, or what you will. It reassures the patients and gives oneself a confidence that is so often painfully lacking.' He paused. 'Unhappily, it is not appropriate for a court of law.'

'I expect it will come out all right, sir, in the end,' I added, still trying hard to cheer him up.

Sir Lancelot made no reply, but reached for an envelope beside him.

'I found this hanging about for you in the porter's lodge at St Swithin's.'

I opened it in silence. It was an invitation to the wedding of Mr Bridgenorth and Miss Miggs.

'And here is your cheque, Grimsdyke. Though after I have faced Mr Justice Fishwick tomorrow, I fear there will be little point in finishing your task. I can only offer my sincere thanks for the work you have performed.'

'It was the least I could have done. After all, sir, mine was one of those lives you saved.'

'What was that?'

'My appendix, sir.'

Sir Lancelot seemed puzzled. 'You mean, you agreed to undertake my memoirs solely because you felt indebted to me for operating on you?'

'The job did rather muck up my work plans, sir,' I confessed. 'But – well, heart-felt gratitude and all that.'

The old boy seemed to be staring at me oddly. 'Grimsdyke, I really must – There's the doorbell,' he broke off. 'Be a good chap and answer it.'

Mr Alphonso Spratt came hurrying into the drawing-room.

'Lancelot, my dear fellow, my dear fellow . . .'

The two brothers shook hands warmly.

'I fear I failed you most miserably this morning, confessed the barrister. 'I lost my temper. It was quite inexcusable.'

'No, Alfie. I should have had sufficient self-control to contain myself while the Judge was being so blatantly unfair.'

'I certainly agree he was outrageously unfair. I really can't understand why. But Fishy has been behaving most oddly these days. Everyone at the Bar has been noticing it.' Sir Lancelot handed him a whisky. 'What was the matter when he collapsed? I know nothing of such things, of course.'

'Purely an attack of colic. He was wise to adjourn the court and go home to bed. Tomorrow morning he will no doubt be in excellent form when he sends the pair of us to prison.'

Alfie shook his head. 'I think if I apologize slavishly enough – and after a night's sleep all round – I shall save our skins in that respect. But your case, I'm afraid, has a pretty bleak outlook.'

'And my career,' agreed Sir Lancelot sombrely. 'I suppose Tiptree will be next President of the Royal College. I must only be grateful that it could never be McFiggie.'

'I'm deeply sorry, Lancelot. Particularly as I don't mind telling you here and now I was confident from the start that we'd win hands down. It was simply that Fishwick jumped in the wrong direction.'

'Perhaps you might win an appeal?' I interjected hopefully.

'I doubt it, young man. They wouldn't reverse Fishwick with no point of law involved.'

'So there's no hope?' ended Sir Lancelot gloomily.

'To be heartlessly frank, none. Only a retrial –'

The doorbell rang again. On the step this time I found Captain Spratt.

'What the devil are you doing here?' he demanded at once.

'Paying a call, sir,' I replied, saluting automatically.

'Where's my brother?'

'In the drawing-room. They both are, in fact.'

The Captain burst in like one of those dinner-table hurricanes of his.

'Lancelot! Alfie! M'dear chap, I was absolutely enraged by the reports in the evening papers. Hell's teeth! The whole business is perfectly scandalous. I came as soon as possible to offer you whatever help it is in my power to give.'

'That is extremely kind of you, George.'

'If we stick together,' agreed Alfie. 'At least we shall be supported through the public clamour by each other's companionship.'

'A pity we have not enjoyed much of it while the years have been eating into our lives,' added Sir Lancelot.

I must say, it was quite a sight, the three Spratts together on the hearth-rug. It had the impressiveness of those old Victorian naval reviews.

Captain Spratt took some snuff.

'It is perhaps not quite the moment to announce another item of news,' he said, glancing round quickly, 'but I must confess I find it somewhat difficult to contain myself.'

The brothers looked at him questioningly.

'In short – Alfie, Lancelot – I have just got married.'

'Married?' we all exclaimed at once.

'Yesterday morning.' Captain Spratt gave a laugh. 'Indeed, I am at this moment on my honeymoon. We are leaving for a voyage on the *Capricorn Queen* tomorrow afternoon. As passengers, naturally.'

'But my dear George!' Sir Lancelot looked confused. 'My congratulations, of course. I can only assure you that Alfie and I are most anxious to meet our new sister-in-law –'

'My wife is in the car outside. The young doctor might have the kindness to show her in.'

Ophelia made a very pleasant impression all round.

'You may also be surprised to hear that I am leaving the Capricorn Shipping Company,' the Captain declared a few minutes later. 'You know how I hate the sea? I shall be going into partnership with my wife in a modelling agency.'

Sir Lancelot spilt his drink.

'Modelling, did you say, George?'

'Yes, I thought they were mad when the Company started taking my photograph months ago. But for some reason my face comes out like a school treat. Now the advertising wallahs have decided these homely features are just the ticket to persuade people to buy things – soap and corned beef and dog biscuits and so on. 'Captain Spratt Recommends –' they're going to put all over the place, God help 'em. Not that I care. The work's easy and the money's good. There's another seafaring feller doing it already in New York, advertising ginger-pop. Now we must be going, my dear –'

'Just one moment,' I interrupted.

'Yes, dar . . . doctor?' said Ophelia.

'I – I happened to hear about your marriage. Secret sources of information, you know. I thought I'd like to give you a little wedding present.'

I unloaded Basil's bracelet.

There was naturally a good deal of cooing over the diamonds, and as we reached the front step the Captain drew me aside for a second.

'By the way, doctor,' he said quickly. 'I know, of course, that both you and that other feller – what's his name? the steward – were at one time both quite attached to my lady. I hope you will forgive me?'

'Nothing to forgive. Jolly good luck to you, and lots of –'

'That is not quite the point.' Captain Spratt lowered his eyes. 'I am conscious of it now – indeed, I may perhaps remain conscious of it for many years of my married life – that I have behaved towards you both as ... as a bit of a cad. Good night!'

Alfie left soon afterwards. I pocketed my cheque and prepared to leave, calculating how long it would keep me in my basement if I went easy on the first-class proteins.

'There is just one thing, Grimsdyke.'

'Sir?'

Sir Lancelot stuck his hands under his coat tails then paced up and down for a moment in silence.

'I have something rather painful to confess to you, my boy.'

'To confess to *me*, sir?'

He nodded.

'Your appendix –'

'Which jolly near did for me –'

'On the contrary, Grimsdyke. I removed a perfectly normal organ.'

I gasped. 'Normal, sir?'

'I made a mistake in diagnosis. It has occurred before and will most certainly occur again. That is all there was to it.'

'But what about all that frightful pain and symptoms –'

'Entirely psychological. Like – er, Possett. Pseudo-appendicitis, very common among doctors and nurses, when undergoing periods of stress. I should have known better. However, it seemed best not to complicate your condition by informing you of the truth, so I concealed it. Indeed, I had a word with a psychiatrist before you recovered from the anaesthetic, and he urged me to withhold the news. He remembered from St Swithin's that you – you will understand I am now speaking purely as your doctor? – that you had a rather weak personality. One too easily bent to the wills of others. I seem to recall he described you as "A psychological balloon." I felt at the time it was better that you should not know.'

'Yes, of course, sir,' I said slowly.

I felt wretchedly disillusioned. And I'd helped him take those ruddy children to the Zoo, too.

'Now I fear I have detained you long enough –'

The telephone rang.

'Spratt here. Hello? Who? Oh, Potter-Phipps. How are you? Yes, of course I know Mr Justice Fishwick. That's the one. I didn't know he was one of yours ... H'm ... Indeed? ... Sounds like a barn-door case to me. Generalized abdominal rigidity? Right. I'll be straight over.'

Sir Lancelot put down the telephone. He seemed to have suddenly cheered up no end.

'Grimsdyke –'

'Sir?'

'I should be obliged if you would kindly telephone the St Swithin's private block and tell them to prepare for a case of perforated peptic ulcer. You may inform the theatre staff that I shall be operating in one hour from now.'

'I say, jolly good! That means a new trial – I mean, I'm frightfully sorry for the poor old judge –'

Sir Lancelot smiled. 'Then kindly ring my usual anaesthetist. You might ask him to remind me to explain to the patient exactly what I think is wrong with the feller before I get my knife in him. Which is more than the blasted man ever did to me.'

Sir Lancelot won his case the following week before another judge, and looks extremely well in the robes of the President of the Royal College of Surgeons. Captain Spratt now chortles at everyone from their cornflake packets over breakfast. The Bishop, I hear, has been inquiring about the healthfulness of the air in Canterbury.

I went back to the basement. I hadn't got much further with the great novel when Basil opened as Hamlet, and was a whacking success. I didn't even get any free seats.